THE LUST LIST: DEVON STONE

FIRST TASTE

MIRA BAILEE

NoMi Press

Euphoria Publishing
NoMi Press
www.euphoriapublishing.com

Publisher's Note: This is a work of fiction. Names, characters, places, and incidents are a product of the author's imagination, and any resemblance to actual people, living or dead, or to businesses, companies, events, institutions, or locales is completely coincidental.

ISBN-13: 978-0692307601
ISBN-10: 0692307605

CHAPTER ONE

I start the morning on a promising note—a full-blown panic attack with a side of desperation.

"Maddie!"

I rush across the living room to the other bedroom in our little apartment. This old place was the best we could afford on our measly incomes in this part of Los Angeles, but we've done our best to spruce it up: scrubbed mildew from the floorboards, strategically placed rugs over the worst of the carpet stains, and I even dedicated my unemployed free time to DIY projects I found online to decorate the bland, beige walls. I'm certain this place is the nicest unit in the building. I mean, Mr. Harrison downstairs has been bitching for months about a two-foot hole in his bathroom wall. Never mind the fact he doesn't want to admit he caused the damage after the Kings lost in overtime. Yeah, this place isn't *that* bad.

But who cares about the state of our apartment when my heart is threatening to escape through my ribs...and my breakfast is threatening to escape through my throat?

Deep breaths.

The jittery feeling persists while I knock on my roommate, Maddie's, door. It swings open with the lightest touch. Her room is dark, and I can hear soft snores coming from the bed.

"Maddie. Wake up. I need you," I say, shaking her foot that hangs out from under the cover.

She groans and rolls over, croaking out an unintelligible slur of words. "It's too early, Olivia. Get the hell out."

My hand goes to my belly, trying to soothe the nauseous feeling. "It's almost noon," I say, tripping over a bag as I walk to the window and pull aside the thick blackout curtains. Harsh sunlight bursts through the thin glass; one of the panes is cracked. Maddie's room illuminates to show off the details that reflect her personality. Dirty laundry strewn about the floor and fast food containers on every surface compete with the intricate silk scarves she has draped over lamps and the string of white Christmas lights woven around the curly iron of her headboard. Maddie is Bohemian-chic meets messy-frat-boy.

In her defense, she does work long hours late into the night bartending at Brecken's Sports Pub. She brings home enough money to help the charity case that is yours truly, covering the rent while I continue my unsuccessful hunt for a job. I'm eternally grateful for her, and I swear I leave her alone most mornings. But today's an important one, and I need Maddie's help.

She's sitting up, assembling her wavy blond hair in a knot on top of her head. Aside from the wreck she resembles when she first wakes up, Maddie is hot—like some perfect combination of classy Academy Award winner and a golden-haired Sports Illustrated swim-suit model, both of which she'd die to be.

"What's wrong?" she asks.

"I need you to help me get dressed."

"Seriously?" She flops back down in bed.

Okay, yes. That sounds pathetic. I'll admit it. But my grandmother has better style than I do, and my closet's filled with clothes that are either worn out from over-washing or two sizes too small. Since my broke ass can't do anything to change what's in there, I have to rely on Maddie—and her talent for making me into a better version of myself—to get me looking like the ideal candidate for Platinum Planning's newest assistant to the head event planner himself, Mr. Greg Keenly. If I land this job, I'll finally make enough money to take care of myself *and* pay Maddie back for everything she's done for me.

"Please. I'm going to end up late if I don't figure this out now, and all I have are ill-fitting, ugly-ass adult clothes."

"You *are* an adult."

"Sure. But I'm twenty-two, and nothing I own looks like it came from the twenty-first century. I need to look good—better than good."

Maddie stumbles out of bed and follows me back to my room. She takes one glance at the outfits laying on my bed—a faded, blue pant-suit and a dress that would better fit a twelve-year-old. Her burst of laughter confirms I need help, and I'm not even offended.

"I told you."

"What's it for? Is it a date? Oh, please tell me it's a date. You so desperately need to get laid. You—"

"It's a job interview."

Maddie's shoulders drop, losing some of her temporary excitement. Of course she would be more worried about me dating than working. My last boyfriend, Bryce, and I broke up over a year ago, and I haven't bothered looking for anyone new. It's too stressful. Dating, the expectations, the whole act of coming across like perfect girlfriend material. More often than not, it just makes me sick. Literally. Being single has its perks. Sure, I'm missing out on potentially decent sex—a momentary relief from my own neurotic nuances, quiet time for my constantly worrying mind. But along with the sex comes the overanalyzing and suspicions and the arguments caused by both. In the end, the guy gets sick of it fast, and I can't blame him. It's much easier to remain single.

Maddie leaves the room only to return a minute later carrying a black dress. She holds it out for me, but I'm skeptical.

"Does that really convey professional—"

"You'll be hot. But not slutty. Put it on." She thrusts it out again, and I take it.

I go to our shared bathroom to change, doing a double take when I see my reflection in the mirror.

"Damn." I can admit this dress gives the right impression. My dark hair frames my face before cascading over my shoulders, detracting from the obvious cleavage this dress gives me. It's formfitting and low-cut but in a way that says 'professional businesswoman' and not 'amateur stripper'. I may even be able to play off confidence if I can get control over the nervous ache in my stomach.

In my room, Maddie is half asleep on my bed. My little square of home is much cleaner than hers but holds little personality. She lifts a hand to point at the side table that holds a simple, white lamp and my charging cell phone. "It was buzzing. I turned it off."

"That means it's time to go." I slip into black flats—no way do I want to deal with heels when I'm feeling all shaky. I'm reaching for my phone when I see Maddie glaring at me. "What?"

"You set an alarm to tell you when to leave?"

"And when to wake up. When to get ready. And a half dozen others to keep me on time today." I grab my purse, unplug my phone, and pull up the map with the directions already routed out. "You shouldn't be surprised."

"I just thought you were working on being less...obsessed with order. Didn't Dr. Shannon—"

"I've gotten better." My therapist has been working on helping me let go of minor control issues in an effort to help me deal with some of the bigger ones. Lately, we've been working on time and my tendency to have everything planned out by the minute. My handy alarms keep me on track, but she says they make me too dependent on outside forces. Days when I'm not busy, I do okay leaving my comfort zone—turning off the alarms and ignoring the clocks—but anticipating today triggered the panic, so I had to give in. Just today. "I see her later. I'll let her know I've been bad."

Maddie sighs, "You're going to be great. Whatever the job is."

"Thank you." I rush over to give her a hug, knowing I need to be in my car in the next thirty seconds. "And thank you for this." I gesture at my dress. "Love you, best friend."

I leave the room as she rolls over in my bed, and I suspect she's not going to bother going back to her own.

Twenty minutes later, when I should be pulling up to the Platinum Planning office, I'm, instead, parked at the security gate of some ritzy housing complex. The guard approaches my window, and I'm not sure what to do next.

"Olivia Margot," I say. "I'm here for an interview at 214 N. Holloway Court."

This guy is inspecting me up and down, a smug grin forming on his face. He's huge—

I'm talking Incredible Hulk's nephew huge. He'd tower about two feet over my five-two frame, and I imagine he has to be cautious when hugging his loved ones so as not to accidentally strangle them. His tan skin glistens from a layer of sweat, yet the heat doesn't seem to faze him as he leans down by my window. I shrink into my seat.

"You must be here to see the old man then. He's clearly got a type with you women..."

He's not so subtle as he glances at my chest, and I suddenly remember the low cut dress. Wait. What? Does he think I'm here as a hooker or something? It's midday...on a Monday. Who—?

I fumble to defend myself. "No. I—uh—that's not. I'm here for something else. A real interview. For a *job*."

His smile proves he doesn't believe me, and he steps back from my car. "Have a good day, ma'am. Good luck with that job."

He presses a button inside the little, brick guard station, and the massive gate, adorned with a big letter 'S', swings open. I try to slow my pulse as I follow the only road that leads the way in. *Relax and pretend you're going to the beach. Just focus on the scenery.* The narrow road is lined with tall, meticulously pruned hedges, and beyond them, I can see the tops of palm trees and evergreens. There aren't any houses or side roads or... This isn't a neighborhood. It's one person's property.

The road—driveway—curves up ahead, and as I get closer I see the scene open up before me. A vast, green lawn seems to appear out of nowhere, and the driveway transitions from gray concrete to a mosaic of bricks and stones. It forms a loop at the end, winding its way around a marble fountain, putting on a water show for no audience. In the distance, the ocean meets the horizon. There's nothing but blue out there, but even that secluded chunk of the world—from the depths of the water straight up into the sky above—doesn't seem to compare to the massive mansion standing before me.

"Holy shit."

CHAPTER TWO

I'd like to say I don't end up driving three times around the fancy fountain, trying to figure out the appropriate place to park, but yeah, that's me. I finally notice where the driveway extends to one side of the house, and I pull up behind the only other car I see. It's a freshly waxed, black Lexus—a shiny onyx compared to the faded denim-color of my twenty-year-old Saturn. I get out of the car but can't bring myself to take a step closer to the monstrous structure in front of me. Where am I? Whose house is this? Glancing at the screen of my phone, I have eight minutes to go. My nerves are still too unreliable to go inside early. I need to feel relaxed enough to know I won't go in and vomit right in front of my interviewer.

It's quiet out here with the peaceful sounds of the Pacific Ocean coming from the frigging backyard. The soothing rhythm of the crashing waves draws me to it, and I walk around the back corner of the house to see what, I assume, is a spectacular sight.

Like something out of a dream, the view is unimaginable. A stone patio leads to an infinity pool that appears to drop straight into the ocean. An iron, spiral staircase leads the way to a second level upstairs, and beyond that one, other similar balconies extend out the back of the house. I'm jealous of whoever gets to leave their room and immediately enter a paradise. I try to stay out of direct view of the enormous windows spanning the walls along the back of the mansion as I make my way closer to the far end of the pool. A short, hidden stairway brings you down to the beach level where these people seem to have this part of Mother Nature all to themselves.

I'd do anything to live in a place like this. I don't need to even go inside. I'd be happy pitching a tent right there on the sand. Fall asleep to the whooshing sound of the water. Wake up to the salty, clean air of a new day...

There. Now I feel at ease, like I can handle today.

"Are you lost?"

I almost jump out of my skin as I whirl around to see who's interrupted my moment of serenity.

One look at him, and I'm right back to square one. My throat catches, and I feel my palms clamming up.

This guy is unbelievably gorgeous. Tall, dark hair, piercing blue eyes, and he's dressed like...like he belongs here. I sure as hell don't, and I'm feeling that certainty increase by the second. If this is his house, then he figured out life long before me. I just graduated with a bachelor's in Hospitality and can't snag a job to save my life. I end up with shitty, part-time gigs just to scrape by. Food service instead of a flourishing career. A run-down apartment instead of a... I look around at this magnificent mansion and the beautiful man standing before me.

He's holding a suit jacket, and the navy blue tie around his neck is loose and framing a white dress shirt, its top button undone. Please tell me this is Mr. Keenly. I'll do my best not to screw up if I can just get a chance to work for this guy.

But who am I kidding? I'm not even talking to him now as he stands there with a confused expression on his face.

"Um...sorry. No, I'm—uh—actually here to meet with Mr. Keenly. Is that you?"

"God, no. That's the asshole planning Saturday's party. You working for him?" He checks me out, furrowing his brow, and I'm reminded of the creep at the front gate.

Of course he's not a party planner. He's got to be a model or something. I'm an idiot for asking. "No. Not yet anyway. I'm supposed to have an interview... But I may have changed my mind."

As inviting as he is in appearance, he seems to be tense. Maybe even angry. His fist clenches a phone, and he pushes his loose hair away from his face. However it had been styled this morning, it's disheveled now, like he just got done fighting with someone or having sex... A vulgar image flashes across my mind. Him. Me. My back up against a wall.

Snap out of it, O.

Is he mad at me? Did I insult him? I check my phone to see I have two minutes left. It'll buzz at 12:30, yet I still feel the need to double check in case I set the wrong alarm or my phone decided to malfunction. You never know.

Right now, I want to flee. Forget the interview. I can't stand out here any longer making an ass out of myself. I can just leave.

Maddie can help me with rent...again, and I'm sure I can find a job at some chain restaurant or a motel needing an overnight concierge. Something low-key, simple. I'm certain if I stick around, what's waiting for me inside will be anything but low-key *or* simple.

I realize from an outside perspective, I'm just standing here, fidgeting and staring at the tan skin peeking out from under my hot stranger's shirt collar. He's clearly noticed, and a mischievous grin replaces his former scowl.

"So you changed your mind? Want to bail?" He glances up toward a window and returns his gaze to me. "If you need an excuse to get out of the interview, I can fill your schedule with something else..."

What is he talking about? He doesn't even know me. Is it the dress? Dammit, I look easy, don't I? Thanks a lot, Maddie. But what kind of guy just puts it all out there like that?

I turn and start toward the door right as my phone begins vibrating. If I have to choose between responding to that obvious come-on and dealing with an awkward job interview, then I'll go find Mr. Keenly now.

"So what's your name?"

This guy is walking alongside of me, not taking my silence as a hint.

"Huh? I have to go in now."

"I just asked your name. If you can't answer that then, damn, this interview's going to suck for you."

I laugh but try to stifle it. I shouldn't encourage him. I'm getting some serious weird vibes from him, like he's used to getting anything he wants. With a face and body like that, I can imagine it's the truth.

"My name's Olivia. Margot."

"Well, Olivia. Good luck to you." We've reached the huge double doors at the front of the house, and he opens one for me. "I'm sure I'll see you around."

We step inside, and the look on his face shifts. His eyes turn cold, and he marches upstairs. So he *is* mad. But, thankfully, not at me. I'm not sure I'd want to be on his bad side. Then again, I'm not sure I want to be on his good side either. His presence is over-whelming, and he demands attention. I imag-ine dating him would be exhausting.

Dating? No. I'm here for an interview.

"Miss Margot, correct?" A stubby, well-dressed man is waiting in a doorway to my right. I rush over realizing I may officially be late thanks to Mr. No-Name.

I reach out my hand to shake his. This guy will be much easier to talk to now that I've survived the encounter with that anonymous male model. *You've got this girl. Now kick some interview ass.*

"Thank you so much for meeting with me."

"Yes, I see you found the place alright—"

"This is bullshit!" Stomping footsteps in-terrupt us as Mr. Hunk follows an older, white-haired man back down the stairs. The old man is dressed in a robe—in the middle of the day—and seems to be nursing a glass of scotch, but I can see from their scowls alone, they're father and son. So I assume he's *the* old man according to the gate guard. "You and Kaidan know what you're doing, and you're screwing me over in the meantime."

He follows him into another room across the foyer, slamming the door behind them. Their arguing continues, muffled through the walls.

Mr. Keenly rolls his eyes. "Let's speak in here where it's quieter."

CHAPTER THREE

"Does that happen a lot?" I motion to the chaos coming from the other room. Dreamy guy is still yelling, and I'm more intrigued by that than the impending interview. I gulp and remind myself I need to focus on the task at hand so I don't blow it.

"You haven't worked with them before? This family is intense, so brace yourself."

I follow him into an office. I can't help but be mesmerized by the mere size of everything. From the chandelier back in the entryway to the massive desk taking up the center of this room, I'm certain all of my belongings would fit in a single closet in this house—with plenty of room for myself and my growing doubt.

I feel torn. This is the nicest house I've ever been in, and to work in it... A part of me still wants to run. This is too much. I don't belong.

"Welcome to my office away from my office. I do so many parties here, I just work in the residence while I'm planning. Makes it easier to get all the details right."

"Of course." Here we go. There's no getting out of it now.

Mr. Keenly motions toward a desk, and I sit across from him in a plush, upholstered chair. I could nap in this thing. The desk is shiny and free of dust and clutter, and a massive paperweight looks out of place holding down a scrawny stack of notes. It could probably be better used anchoring a ship. Keenly snatches a pen from a marble cup and begins knocking it against the surface of the desk. *Tap, tap.*

"So a little about the job," he begins. I focus on my breathing as I listen. *In, out. In, out.* "I coordinate a variety of events here and around the city. I'm a very busy man and have garnered high respect, so I'm seeking out an assistant who can, essentially, help me be in two places at once. An assistant must be able to make decisions on my behalf. They must possess excellent judgment and a professional image."

I'm distracted by his tapping but so far, I think I can handle all this.

He continues, "At Platinum Planning, we're an all-inclusive event planning agency. We have our own in-house catering division with renowned chefs and experienced staff. We handle furnishings, decorating, scheduling, and, of course, event day coordination. Our events are flawless—always have been under my watch. Does this sound like a position for which you'd excel?"

Think carefully. This could be a dream job. "Absolutely. Without a doubt. I—"

"Do you feel you possess the aptitude to make swift, flawless decisions?"

Aptitude? Yes. Ability? Well, I don't have the cleanest record. I tend to overthink and screw up. "I'm very diligent when it comes to details and have excellent insight that will help ensure my decisions align to what you would expect." *So far, so good, O.*

"Alright. And tell me about how well you interact with others. How are you with large crowds, high-profile guests, your confidence as a hostess?"

My nails dig into the arm of the chair as the thought alone—of catering to important people, of having their attention on me—brings back the same thumping in my chest as before. "Good." My voice cracks, and I clear my throat. "I mean, I'm good in social situations. Have no problem with them."

Mr. Keenly eyes me with suspicion as he continues his *tap, tapping*. "Tell me about your experience," he says, sifting through a folder with his free hand and pulling out my resumé.

"Well, I received a Bachelors in Hospitality Management, graduating summa cum laude with a perfect 4.0 GPA."

"Mhmm." *Tap, tap. Tap.*

"...And during my last semester I had the honor of interning with Striker Events and Media—"

"And they are?" He's not sounding impressed...at all.

I try to steady my voice. "They host events at a number of country clubs and hotels along the West Coast."

His tapping halts, and now he's glaring down at my resumé as if searching for a secret code. He presses his fingers to the bridge of his nose like he has a sudden headache. "And what did you do as an intern?" The word sounds drenched in animosity.

What did I do? I picked up garbage and wrapped utensils in cloth napkins. I almost choke trying to come up with a spin to make my minuscule experience sound worthy. "I...uh...assisted in the pristine, impeccable design of each event location and ensured the amenities were top quality."

"And were any of these *pristine* events catered to the rich and famous?"

I consider the events I attended. A graduation. Sweet sixteens. A couple of weddings.

"Every one of our clients were high class. And the events were planned and hosted to the...highest of standards. And the guest of honor was our hi—highest focus." Who am I kidding?

Keenly stares at me blankly. Maybe I've pushed the bullshitting too far. My stomach is full of knots, and I'm ignoring the impulse to run away.

"With the highest of my patience being pushed, Miss Margot, I've heard enough."

"No, wait. I—"

He holds his hand up to stop me. "This isn't some middle class, weekend theme party thrown together by some low-rate party planners." The pompous man closes his folder, leaving my resumé lying on the table next to a leather organizer and a gold-plated miniature globe. I'd happily pick any spot on that shiny, tiny world to disappear to right this second. "We're talking Hollywood elite here. You're in the midst of American royalty. And it takes more than some intern to pull off the quality of events that take place in this very residence. You have to keep up, and quite frankly, I'm far from convinced that you—"

"But sir, I can do it. I know I don't... I may not be..." There has to be something I can say to redeem myself. "Please. I can prove—"

"You have to be kidding. Begging will not get you any points here." He looks toward the closed office door and then down at his watch. "I'm on a tight schedule. There are other interviews. Other candidates. Many of which who've made names for themselves. If you want to work with some of the most influential, important people in this country, I suggest you do the same... Somewhere else."

I'm frozen in place as Keenly picks up my resumé, wads it up, and tosses it into the trashcan near his feet. I bet that thing cost more than my monthly grocery budget. I want to say something, anything, to mend my broken ego, but Keenly clears his throat loudly, and I take it as my cue to leave.

I should've known better. I should've fled when I had the chance. Working here? I'd be an even bigger nervous wreck. Famous people—they're always in the spotlight. Always surrounded by tons of people. Always composed and personable—ready to smile for the cameras with their perfect, bleached teeth. Their lives are beyond anything I can comprehend.

I cower out of the office. *I can see myself out, thanks.* I wish I had the nerve to get into Keenly's face and tell him off. Asshole.

Instead I close the office door behind me and sigh with relief. It's easier to breathe in this vast, open foyer. Floor to ceiling windows invite all the day's light inside. Two marble staircases curve up to the second floor. And an enormous sparkling chandelier hangs from the ceiling resembling an orb of dripping diamonds rather than a light fixture. I think the most expensive lamp in my house cost $30—and the bulb is burnt out.

The door across from me opens, and before I can make my escape, I'm staring into the icy blue eyes of my mystery man. Maybe I can take him up on his offer now. Let him take my mind off my own failures. I'm sure he can distract me. I'm sure he can do all sorts of things to me.

CHAPTER FOUR

He gives me a once-over. "Are you crying?" he asks.

Dammit. I didn't even notice. "No."

I bring my hand to my face to wipe away the trail of tears that's giving away my personal shame. There goes my chance with this guy. Now he can laugh at me, a perfect follow-up to the thorough berating I just endured. And later, an audience will have the opportunity to chuck tomatoes at my face. I'm an all out spectacle.

He walks closer, and I can only imagine the puffy eyes and smudged makeup I'm sporting. He stops in front of me, but instead of leaving any amount of personal space between us, he's standing over me, his tie skimming the front of my dress. I try to look away, but he lifts my chin. His fingers seem to possess an electricity that travels through my body. Without speaking, he takes me in, demanding my eye contact as his own gaze scans my hair, my jaw, my lips, my neck. A shiver runs through me, and a grin reappears on his face. What's so funny?

"Are you always this rigid?"

Oh honey, you don't know the half of it.

I'm in a daze, entranced by his closeness. His cologne smells like lying in tangled sheets in the middle of a field—musky and herbal at the same time. It's intoxicating. I don't know what he wants, but I'm certain I'd do whatever it is.

That thought alone snaps me back to reality, and I step back. What am I doing?

"I take it a congratulations is not in order?" he asks.

Is he going to be rude now too? "I didn't get it. It's fine. I was just leaving."

"Did you want the job?"

I want you. Forget the job. "It's just a job. I can find another."

"That doesn't answer my question. Did you want this one?"

A chance to work in this level of luxury? The chance to see this guy again? Hell yeah, I want it. "Yes."

He walks past me into the office. "Hey, Keenly."

"Devon, my favorite young man..."

Devon. Hot guy has a name now.

Keenly sees me standing behind Devon, and for a moment he glares at me. But he erases his face of any expression and plasters on a practiced smile instead. "What can I do for you?"

"Stop your shit." Devon's voice is calm, but there's an authoritative tone to it that's just as threatening as him storming through the house yelling earlier. "You have a job to do, and as far as I can see, you're wasting my family's time and money fishing around for employees to do your busywork for you. Here's your new hire. Olivia Margot. When do you want her to start?"

Devon reaches back to me, flicking his hand to summon me forward. I take a couple steps, not sure what's going on here.

"With all due respect, sir," Keenly says while struggling to keep his composure. "This woman would not be a valuable asset to your time or money. She has none of the qualifications needed—"

"You work for me, Greg. And now she works for you. Is that clear?" Devon doesn't have to move an inch to seem like he's bearing down on the little man. His tone, alone, seems to be effective. "If you continue to argue, she'll replace you entirely."

Keenly releases an audible sigh but doesn't object any further. Instead, he leans down to grab a briefcase, plopping it onto the desk and sifting through its contents. He pulls out a paper clipped bunch of pages and lays them on the edge of the desk rather than handing them to me directly.

"These need to be filled out. Bring them in tomorrow."

"What time?" I ask, meekly.

"It doesn't matter."

Devon swipes the paperwork off the desk, handing it to me, and just as swiftly, he directs me back out of the office, his hand pressing against the small of my back. Such a casual touch, but his hand sends instant warmth deep into me. I could melt. I don't know where this is heading. It feels like an out-of-body experience.

Back out of the office, Devon heads down a hallway before I can thank him. But I really should thank him, right?

I trace his steps down the hall and through a doorway on the right—the kitchen. He opens the refrigerator, pulling out a beer. A little early for that, in my opinion, but I won't judge the person who just scored me a potential career-building job.

"Hey. Um...Sorry. I just wanted to say thanks." I lean against the doorway, trying to keep my calm. Devon opens the bottle, taking a couple gulps before he even turns toward me.

"You know, if you want to show your thanks..." He looks at me with the same provoking expression he gave me outside.

Does he expect me to return the favor by sleeping with him? "No. Thank you. But. I'm not like th—I don't. I just... You didn't have to do that for me, that's all."

"Oh, I didn't do it for you." He moves toward some cabinets, rummaging through their contents. "I love pissing off that dickwad. He and my dad have been buddy-buddy since their college days. Now he mooches off my father however he can. I figure, if you're any good, then it works out. Cool. But if you're as awful as Greg seems to think you are..." He laughs. "Oh man, that'll make this weekend much more entertaining."

And with that he leaves through another doorway. No goodbye. No more sexual advances. He just leaves, and I'm dumbfounded. I don't know whether to hate him or fantasize about him. And I can't pinpoint how I went from bombing an interview to following this Devon guy around like a schoolgirl chasing after her crush.

It doesn't matter. I got a job. And I'll be seeing more of Devon soon enough.

CHAPTER FIVE

"Olivia. You seem distracted today."

Dr. Maureen Shannon sits across from me in a high-backed armchair, its upholstery a soft pink with little blue birds all over. I'm slouching in her forest green, corduroy love seat, twisting my phone in circles on my lap while my brain replays my interactions with Devon.

"Are you alright?" she asks.

I blink and focus on her. She wears a yellow skirt and jacket over a white, buttoned blouse. Her blond hair is pulled back from her face, and her entire ensemble makes me want to call her Sunshine. "Yeah. I'm fine." I sit up straighter, trying to push out images of Devon—his strong jawline, his smooth skin, his very kissable mouth. "I...um...had another interview today."

"That's wonderful. How did it go?"

Awful. Worse than awful. "It went well. It's a temp job as an assistant to a party planner. I'll be able to afford rent." I'm downplaying the extravagance of it all. I wouldn't know where to start if I tried to describe the mansion and upcoming party and Devon.

"And how do you feel about the job itself? Or rather, how is this job making *you* feel?"

"I'll be working around a lot of people—important people." And Devon. What is his deal? He's nice to me. He hits on me. Then he completely brushes me to the side like I'm...like I'm nothing.

"When you say 'important people', be careful to not belittle your own worth. You're important as well—"

"Um, no. I'll be working with famous people. Rich people. Influential and powerful people." According to what Mr. Keenly claimed, at least. "It wasn't a jab against myself."

"Very well. Tell me how our experiment is going. How have your days been?"

She's talking about my alarms. I don't see what the problem is with them. I grip my phone tighter as I answer. "Fine. I've been fine. Check the clock a lot more often, but it's okay. I did have to turn them on today. But just today."

"And how many did you set?"

I look down at my phone, though I already know the answer. "Eight."

"Can you tell me what they were all for?"

Of course I can. I always can. I recite them in order. "8:00 wake up. 11:00 get ready. 12:00 leave for interview. 12:30 interview. 2:30 leave for this appointment. 3:00 appointment. 5:00 make dinner. 8:00 set tomorrow's schedule." I shouldn't have admitted that last one. This is the closest thing to exposure therapy I've agreed to, and I'd promised I'd try my hardest.

"Do you plan to use them tomorrow?"

I know damn well I will. I have to go back to that mansion in the morning. "No. I don't think so."

"Good. Keep working on that. Next month, I want to discuss the next step I'd like you to try."

"Which would be...?" I don't want to try anything new. If I'm being honest, I don't want to even come here. She's the only person that makes me talk about my brother, Jared. But that's why I keep coming back...*because* she's the only person that makes me talk about him.

"Don't worry about it. For now, you know what we're working on."

Don't worry about it? That's an evil trick. She said that knowing I will worry for the entire next month.

"Can I ask you something?" she says, as though she wouldn't if I said no. "How would the events of your brother's passing have changed if you relied on all these alarms back then?"

She's asked me this before, so I think she's checking to see if my answer's changed. It hasn't. I think back to five years ago.

I'd skipped school to hang out with my friends instead. Tyler and I were dating at the time. He had an older brother who'd sell us weed for unreasonable prices. Then Tyler and I and our little group of friends would hang out in Tyler's pool house wasting away entire days sometimes. And when it was just me and Tyler, those days would be spent naked, getting lost in each other. His tan, Spanish skin. My purple-streaked hair. It was easy to be carefree and spontaneous back then.

It was a Friday, and I was still high when I finally left to pick up my little brother. I'd be late, but fourteen-year-old Jared couldn't do anything about it even if he did get mad. I was doing him the favor. Pulling into the high school, I was too busy thinking up excuses for my teachers in case they noticed me in my car. I didn't notice the cluster of police cars blocking my usual route to the parking lots until I had to slam on my brakes to avoid rear-ending one of them.

"Shit."

I looked around, paranoid. Did anybody see me do that?

That's when I noticed the fire truck. The ambulance. The flashing lights from the cop cars. The 'Do Not Cross' yellow tape. All blocking off the familiar entrance to the woods to the right of the school. So many kids—including myself—took that path leading to a half-assed tree house built by some freshmen several years before. A group of seniors back then had taken it over, and ever since it's where we'd all go to skip a class or smoke a cigarette or compare the tastes of the liquor we'd stolen from our parents, hiding it in our makeshift flasks of lotion bottles and medicine containers. But our safe-haven would never be the same.

I take a deep breath, not wanting to remember the rest. I glance at the clock hanging on the wall near a cheerful inspirational poster encouraging me to persevere. This appointment was so close to being over. Thank god.

As I focus on pushing back all those past feelings and memories, it's like my veins harden and my blood turns cold. I stiffen in my seat and repeat the same truth that's haunted me since I was seventeen.

"If I'd been on time, Jared would still be alive."

CHAPTER SIX

An excited voice greets me from the kitchen. "You get the job?"

I get home right as Maddie is pulling out a freshly nuked pizza from the microwave. She knows I see a therapist, and she knows about my brother, but I made it clear when we first met two years ago that I didn't want to talk about it. Maddie's the type to respect that without pushing it. A part of me is certain it's because she wouldn't know how to react if we did have deep conversations about my past. I've rarely seen a bad day from bubbly, live-for-the-moment Maddie. I'd hate to bring her down with my issues, and instead, I try to live vicariously through her free-spirited nature.

Over the past several months, I've suspected she goes out of her way to form some sort of distraction after my appointments with Dr. Shannon. She never confirmed it, but she's always put extra effort into taking my mind off of everything when I get home. Tonight, she's doing so with pizza.

I set my things on the counter right as my phone buzzes for my 5:00 alarm. Shutting it off, I ignore Maddie side-eyeing me. I grab a cardboard slice of sauce and imitation cheese and plop into a chair instead.

"I did, but it's more complicated than that," I say, burning my tongue on the first bite of my food.

Maddie joins me at the table. She sports a low-cut tank top and jeans that must cut off her circulation, but not only does she pull off the look—heels and all—she is convincingly comfortable on top of it. If I tried to imitate her, I'd come out resembling a suffocating raccoon with 80s hair. I could use a dose of her confidence.

"Speak, woman," she says, kicking me under the table.

How do I summarize the events of this day? Where do I start?

"Well... The interview was at this ridiculous mansion. You should've seen it."

"Ooh," Maddie's eyes widen. "Rich boss?"

"No, it belongs to the family we'll be planning a party for."

"That'll be fun. Do they need a bartender?"

I laugh. "I'll keep my ear out. Unfortunately, the boss is a complete jerk. He wasn't going to give me the job, but Devon—um, one of the guys in this family—insisted I get it."

Maddie stops mid-chew. "Wait. What? What guy?"

Do I describe our up-close-and-personal encounter when he was hovering over me? Or do I tell her how he completely crossed the line of flirting and invited me to sleep with him? Or do I tell her about how he blew me off and left without a word?

"Just some guy."

I try my hardest to keep a straight face, but a rogue smile gives me away. Maddie stares me down waiting for more information.

"It's nothing! I just ran into him before the interview. And then again after. When he found out Keenly—my new boss—had rejected me, he...well, he basically went in and threatened the man."

"Really? But why?" She catches herself and holds her hands up to stop me from misunderstanding her. "I mean, you're awesome, and you'll rock this job, and anyone should know that. But I'm confused. Who is this guy? Someone you knew? Why was he quick to jump to your defense like that?"

I laugh at her excitement, particularly because... "You don't even know what the job is," I say, but I answer so she doesn't have to ask. "I'm now the assistant to the head event coordinator at Platinum Planning."

"I've heard of them before. Nice work."

"And to answer your other questions, the guy's Devon. I've never seen him before—I don't think. I mean, he looked a little familiar, but he's definitely not someone I've talked to before. And he said he did it to piss off my boss."

Maddie arches an eyebrow. "Come on, girl. That's hard to believe. If he didn't know you, and he helped you out like that... It means he thought you were hot. You said he lives in this mansion?"

I ignore her theory. He may have hit on me, but he also made it clear he wasn't doing me a favor. "I don't know if he does. His family does though. He was there fighting with his dad. It's no big deal. It was just a strange encounter. That's all."

"That's far from *all*. You're just getting started." Maddie fumbles through her purse and pulls out her phone. "Where's this mansion? Who are these people?"

"Over by the beach? And I said I don't know. Keenly said they're important. He mentioned pretentious sounding things like 'Hollywood elite' and 'American royalty'. It was incredibly uncomfortable, and you know how I am. I can't handle that sort of attention and limelight. I'd be a blubbering mess—I *was* a blubbering mess. So I don't even know what to expect from this part—"

"You said his name's Devon?"

"Yeah."

She taps at her phone screen and listens to me simultaneously. I'm used to this conversational multitasking with her. "And he's from a rich family who throws frequent Hollywood parties?"

"That's pretty much everyone who's anyone in this city, but yeah. What's your point?"

"Is this your knight in shining armor—the guy who just defended your honor so you'd work in his home?"

She holds her phone out for me to see. It's open to some tabloid site. I squint to read the smaller print. *ScandalLust Magazine.*

The Lust List.

3. Devon Stone.

And then there's a photo. Wet hair. Unbuttoned shirt. A body I can't describe without wanting to touch it—toned chest, defined abs, low-rise jeans that make my imagination do embarrassing things. And those piercing blue eyes.

Oh my god.

It's him. Devon. And I feel like I'm seeing something I shouldn't. Something private, but it's posted online. And he's apparently one of "the most desired bachelors in the world".

I have no words.

"Liv? Is this him?"

I meet her gaze, and the little bit of pizza I've eaten is threatening to make a reappearance. I nod my head slowly.

"Holy shit. You aren't lying." She gives a little squeal and stomps her heels against the scratched linoleum floor.

I shake my head no. I couldn't make this up if I tried. But why did he—what did he see in me?

"You struck gold today, girl. What are you going to do?"

"Is it too late to decline the job offer?"

"Oh hell no. Look at this." She holds the phone out again but twists it back so she can stare too. "The things I could do..."

"Maddie!"

"Sorry. The things *you* could do."

I glare at her. "You realize how ridiculous this is. Today must have been some fluke. A guy like that? They don't go for girls like me. I'm sure he has a supermodel girlfriend or something."

"Says right here, 'Good news, ladies. Devon is currently single. Better act fast. It won't be for long.' Hear that? Better act fast, Liv."

I stand up, no longer hungry, and dump the rest of my pizza into the trashcan while Maddie reads random facts from her phone. "'Devon Stone—of the Stone Record Label mass empire is up against his twin brother, Kaidan, to take over the reins when their father—and founder of the label—retires next year.' Ew, you realize that guy is super old and dating Serena Lynn?"

"That sounds like it'll last." Serena Lynn is the current trend of the music charts. Every single seems to be huge before it even hits the radio. Meanwhile, she's in a relationship with someone who could be her grandfather.

"Anyway," Maddie continues. "Devon's twenty-eight and the notorious bad boy of the family...Last serious girlfriend was Tempest Ultra singer, Kennedy Rose, but they broke up two years ago. Now he prefers one-night stands and disappearing from the spotlight for weeks at a time. Ooh, maybe you can disappear with him. Wonder where he goes..."

"You know how hard it was to speak to him? Could you imagine me dating him?"

Maddie contemplates it for a second. I'm sure she knows me well enough to know I'm not celebrity girlfriend material. *Girlfriend?* Why am I even thinking these terms? Maddie's revelation about him makes it even more apparent we're from vastly different worlds. I work for him. Period.

I respond to Maddie's continued silence. "Exactly. Nothing will happen. Hell, I'll try to get you into the party, and you can date him. You could make it down a red carpet without tripping."

"As much as I like the challenge, I have a feeling I'd much rather watch how this all pans out for you."

I snatch up the new hire paperwork and retreat to my room. I'd bombed the interview. I should've left quicker. Now, I can't comprehend what I've gotten myself into.

CHAPTER SEVEN

I'm struggling to fill out these forms. It's all basic information about taxes and depositing my paychecks and confidentiality agreements, but my mind is reeling from everything Maddie just told me.

Devon Stone.

He'd been inches from my face. He'd given me an open invitation to have sex with him. And I find out he's actually *somebody*?

Pushing the paperwork aside, I open my laptop and type 'Devon Stone' into an online search engine. Maddie had figured him out so easily. What else did I not know about him?

The image results show me a collection of candid and modeled shots of Devon. Some fully dressed. Others...not so much. There's even a photo of him in a tux standing with his brother. Kaidan is the same level of sexy, and I can't help but wonder how many women have tried to hook up with both hot twins.

Below the images are news articles, mostly from trashy tabloid sites. I'm afraid to click on any of them as I read through their headlines.

"Devon Stone Arrested Again. You Won't Believe What He Did This Time"

"Rose May Have the Key to His Heart, But Who's Got the Key for the Cuffs?"

"Stone Pulled Over, Friend Taken in for Cocaine Possession"

I slam the laptop shut and try not to think about it as I grab clothes and head toward the shower. I'm calling it an early night. If that's just the tip of the iceberg with Devon, I have no interest in finding out the rest.

In the bathroom, I start the water and take a long look at myself in the mirror. Why would he come on to me? I'm not hideous, but I couldn't be more ordinary. My long, auburn hair's been cut recently enough that it still has some bounce. And I've always favored how my eyes are more gray than blue. Otherwise, I'm not much for makeup, and I'm not as fit as I wish I were. But Devon didn't seem to care, so that should boost my confidence a little.

I undress and step into the shower, focusing on clearing my mind. But I can't stop thinking about him.

He'd be awful for me—not that he's the kind of guy seeking a relationship. His proposition today proved that. But even if it were just a fling, it would require me to completely let go of who I am. I'd no longer be in control, I'm sure of it. Just as I'm certain he doesn't play by the rules.

The hot water runs down my skin and steams up the bathroom as I shampoo my hair. I'm finding it hard to breathe. But instead of nerves, it's from the images of Devon I can't get out of my head. The photos of him half-naked and so serious. So powerful. And the headlines. His strange behavior with me. He's a risk taker. He's reckless.

He's trouble.

What would it be like to be with him? To have that confidence, that self-assurance on top of me, staring down at me intently as he thrusts in and out and...

I reach down and spin the temperature knob to cold.

Maybe in another life.

But in this one, Devon Stone couldn't be more wrong for me.

When I return to my room, I feel more flustered than when I left. Sitting at my desk, I glance at the half-filled forms, then at my closed laptop. Then back to the forms. I grab my phone opting, instead, to schedule my day tomorrow. An alarm to wake up. One to leave.

But I don't know what else I'm doing tomorrow. I hate not being able to plan for it, so I set one more for 11:15 to sit down and add any others. They keep me on track. I don't care what Dr. Shannon says. They're harmless, and they help me.

Messing with my phone only wasted a minute of this night, and I find myself staring at the fruit-shaped inlay on top of my closed laptop. I open it, and the search results for Devon are still on the screen. Unable to contain my curiosity, I open the one that stood out to me the most:

"Rose May Have the Key to His Heart, But Who's Got the Key for the Cuffs?"

Our favorite bad boy of the Stone Empire is making headlines again. Devon Stone can't seem to settle down even now that he has the beautiful Kennedy Rose (Tempest Ultra) faithfully at his side.

This article is from over two years ago. A picture to the right shows Devon with his hair a little longer than it was today and subtle facial hair that makes his jawline even stronger. Next to him, a gorgeous woman smiles. She has spunky, short hair dyed pitch black and porcelain skin covered in bold makeup. It's obvious she's a rock star, and I could never follow that act. She's stunning and exudes personality. *She* could handle Devon.

I scroll down, skimming through the article hoping to learn more about "the key to his heart".

Even Rose can't tame this one. On Saturday, June 2, she and Stone were on a flight to Miami when a First Class fight broke out. Stone was taken into custody after allegedly starting a physical altercation with another passenger. He managed to get one punch in before air marshals restrained them. Stone remained under the marshals' supervision until the plane landed safely at its original destination.

It goes on to explain how Calvin Stone, his father, flew over in his private jet to bail him out, but I'm more distracted by the photo that's appeared on the left.

A very angry Devon Stone. Handcuffed. A solemn look on his face as he's being escorted by someone in a uniform.

I don't know why this appeals to me. But Devon's messy hair. His clenched jaw. The metal restraints forcing his hands behind his back.

I feel an ache deep inside as I look at him and think back to how close he was to me earlier.

And how I'll see him again tomorrow.

I'm entirely too turned on by this.

CHAPTER EIGHT

The paperwork may be ready, but I certainly am not. I'm wearing another one of Maddie's dresses, this one's light blue with short sleeves, and I'm reminded I have no idea what I'm going to wear to the party itself. Standing in front of the mirror, I fix my hair for the twentieth time and double check that my tinted lip-gloss isn't on my teeth.

My breath is minty fresh. I remembered antiperspirant. I even put a couple coats of matte gray on my nails.

"You remember you're just going to work right?" Maddie appears in the bathroom doorway, eyeing me suspiciously.

Yesterday was spent convincing myself, with clear proof to substantiate it, that Devon and I would never work. But this morning, I seem to have woken up with amnesia. The mere thought that I might run into him again is sending waves of exhilaration through my veins. And I'm nervous as hell.

My heart flutters, and an involuntary smile gives me away.

"...Unless you're planning on following through on some other scheme?" Maddie says.

"What? No. Just work." I push past her and go to my room to finish getting ready. "Don't overthink it, Maddie," I call to her.

"I don't think I'm the one you need to tell that to."

I slip on my only pair of heels—it's a risky move but it completes the ensemble—and I grab my purse, checking the mirror one last time. I look good. Definitely dateable—I mean, professional.

I move toward the front door. I'm eager to leave even with my heart palpitating like crazy. My phone buzzes right as my hand touches the door handle. *Right on time.*

"And turn off your—"

I shut the door behind me, interrupting Maddie in mid-sentence. Doesn't she know I need to get to work?

Getting through the gates yesterday was a mild obstacle. Today, I see it's going to be a spectacle. A line of cars are parked on the side of the road, and a half-dozen people—loaded with cameras and microphones—are harassing the security guard. Since these people are blocking my way, I tap my horn to get them to step aside. Big mistake.

They move, sure. And I'm able to approach the closed gate. But they swarm to my window, blinding me with camera flashes. I throw my hands over my face like I'm escaping a bad dream. Panic fills me from inside, and I feel lightheaded like I'm experiencing déjà vu. What do they want with me?

I can't control my own trembling as someone taps persistently on my window. I peek out expecting to be ambushed by flashes. Instead, the guard has pushed his way through to speak to me. He looks annoyed until brief recognition crosses his face. "The girl from yesterday?"

"Olivia Margot." My voice wavers. "I work here now—for Greg Keenly."

I'm trying to regain my composure as he nods, seeming much friendlier and less intimidating today. "Alright, let me call up front. Then I'll need to get all these vultures back so you can get through without them making a break for it."

If this is what it's like to be a rich and famous Hollywood celebrity, I'm definitely not interested.

The guard appears again. "As soon as I get them all across the street, I'll buzz you in. Be quick."

"Why are they here?"

"This time?" he says, scratching the side of his nose. "Could be the party. People are hearing about it. Could be the boys in the tabloids. They tend to bring attention to themselves."

The Lust List. I nod my head in agreement as though I know as much as the next celebrity gossip queen about the Stone brothers. "Well, I'm ready when you are," I say.

He reaches a thick, dark hand into the car to shake mine. "The name's Roger, by the way. Welcome to the Stone Circus."

As promised, Roger gets everyone back far enough that when he opens the gate for me, they won't have enough time to race through as well. It would be comical in theory, but the fact this is really happening... Don't these people have better things to do?

I speed through the gate and notice I feel more confident as I near the house. It could be the adrenaline from getting to pass all those camera people, gaining access to the residence with no trouble. *That's right, you jerks. I'm important too.* Or maybe it's because I know Devon could be inside. But I'm feeling good, as if, for this moment, I belong here. Today, I will revel in the luxury of this massive estate. I could never handle the lifestyle, but for this short stint as the Stone's event planner, I'll at least try to take advantage of the perks that come with extreme wealth.

I'm standing on the front steps, knocking on the door, when I hear another car driving up. A vintage muscle car comes around the corner—midnight blue with white racing stripes. My best guess, it's a Camaro from the 60s, but its condition is flawless. It rumbles to a stop by the fountain, and where most would say the car itself was pretty sexy, it's nothing compared to how hot Devon looks getting out of it.

Yesterday, he was professional: suit and tie and all Gucci model-like. Today, he's wearing

a t-shirt that's thin and tight enough to clarify the photo I saw on *ScandalLust* wasn't dig-
itally altered. His jeans are torn—and not,
like, pre-torn for fashion's sake. They're worn
out and older, like they're that favorite pair
you can't just let go of after years of abuse.
This laid-back look is even more effective
than yesterday. Yesterday, he was an inacces-
sible daydream. Today, he's an irresistible
boy next door. He disappears around a corner,
and I extend my neck trying to see where he
went. I have the urge to follow him. This isn't
good. I have work to do.

My jaw's still hanging as I'm abruptly
pulled back into reality.

"Excuse me, Miss Margot." An impatient,
sharp tone comes from Mr. Keenly who's
standing in the doorway with a constipated
scowl on his face.

"Sorry. Hi," I say, handing him my paperwork. "I've got this all filled out for you, and
I—"

"Here." He thrusts a torn sheet of paper at me. "This is what you're doing today. You don't need to be here."

"Oh. All right. Thank—" He shuts the door.

Dammit. Right as Devon gets here, I have to leave.

I do an about-face on the steps, and read the paper Keenly gave me.

1.   Opulent Couture on San Vicente (pick up)

2.   Eco Clean Dry Cleaner on Melrose (drop off)

Drop off what?

Just as I think it, the front door opens again to reveal Keenly holding a massive pile of silky, cream-colored fabric. I barely have time to reach out before he dumps everything into my arms. They're heavy as hell, but at least I have my answer.

I trudge back to my car, unlock the back door, and dump the contents of my arms onto the backseat. So the guy gives me two vague locations with even vaguer instructions. I guess he hasn't gotten over yesterday's incident.

Thankfully, my phone can save the day, and I pull it out to search for the directions to these places. As I'm typing in my first location, a door opens at the side of the house, and there's Devon again.

I can't possibly be this lucky. Keep calm and make casual conversation. *You can do this.*

I lean back against my car, almost falling straight into the backseat. Shifting over, I make sure I look as carefree as he does.

"Hey," I say, but it's too meek. I speak up. "Hi. Devon."

He's walking along the side of the house and stops at a window. "Hey," he mumbles, but doesn't turn to see who's speaking. I'm sure he knows it's me.

"So Keenly's got me running errands today. Thanks again for helping me out."

He turns his head long enough to give me a quick once over, and then turns back. There was no expression on his face, like he didn't even recognize me.

He's peering through half open curtains into the office where I had my interview. What's he looking for? And why is he doing it from out here?

Startled by something, he backs up quickly and stands against the wall out of sight. This is weird, but he's watching me now. He gives me a half-grin and says, "Did Keenly task you with babysitting the driveway?"

I'm feeling smaller by the second. What did I do wrong? What should I say to him? This is definitely not the type of situation where I can just talk about the weather. I've got to sound like I know more about him and his lifestyle. *I totally get you, Devon.* Except I don't—at all. I could make a joke about the Number Three thing...

I'm laughing before I start talking which makes me look like a fool. "So I saw—" No. I can't bring that up! I'd sound like an idiot fan girl. I stand up straight, tempted to just get in my car and leave before anything stupid can come out of my mouth.

But I can't screw this all up now. Taking a breath, I try not to babble. "So it's got to be weird dealing with those camera people all the time." No, I shouldn't have said that. They may have left before he drove up. What if they did? Then I'm making no sense and sound all sorts of crazy.

"Those assholes? They're bloodsucking parasites chasing after their next headline to twist into lies and smut. And those who read it are only feeding them. Like a bunch of ticks growing fatter by feeding off the souls of those trying to live their lives in peace. You don't read that shit do you?"

Not before last night, but now that I know you're all over it... "No. Of course not." I add in a disgusted look to show him I'm serious. I'm so glad I didn't bring up the Lust List thing, and I mentally remind myself to never do so. Ever. "I mean, I don't read any of that. I didn't even know who you were before this job."

"Right." He turns back to check the window, and his shoulders seem to relax.

"I'm sorry. What are you doing?" I ask.

"None of your business. And don't go talking to the paps about anything either. You'll only regret it." He starts back toward the side door in a rush.

"Oh, I wouldn't. I mean. I signed a confidentiality agreement, but even if I hadn't..." Too late. He's inside. Once again, he didn't say goodbye. But worse, I'm not sure he even remembers my name.

CHAPTER NINE

Shake it off. I've been rejected by guys before. This is no different. I should be proud that I was able to get words out of my mouth. Typical Olivia would've found a way to run off and avoid the entire interaction.

But dammit, he's hot. What's his problem? Snooping around his father's house like a burglar. Only giving me the time of day when it's convenient. My head is screaming at me to stay away and not bother. But the rest of my body is intrigued. I want to know him. I want to be closer to him. And those seconds where he pays attention to me—and that grin—it's enough to reinforce all my bad ideas.

Back on my phone, I find the physical addresses I need and get away from the Stone mansion as fast as possible. I'm no longer nervous about running Keenly's errands. They'll give me a chance to regroup before I have to come back.

Five hours, one stop for gas, six wrong turns, and several confused looks later, I'm back at the Stone's. The linens are at the dry cleaners, and I have a box of fancy, handwritten menus and place cards in my backseat. I get out and balance the box on my hip as I walk back to the front door. Today was not the day for heels. I was feeling bold this morning. Now I'm just trying not to limp.

I skip knocking this time, but before I go in, I take a quick scan of the driveway. Devon's car is gone. I guess I feel relieved. At least, I should.

Inside, I take in the quiet, vast space and start down the hallway leading to the back of the house. I assume I'll run into my wonderful boss at some point. He'll probably yell at me for taking so long.

I find a large ballroom that looks like it came out of an animated princess movie. Tables are being set up throughout. Chairs are being polished. A group of people dressed in black and white are surrounding a table of food in the center. A woman in a dark blue pencil skirt and floral blouse has her mouth filled with food as she explains the names of different dishes and what's in them.

All these people bustling about and not a Keenly in sight.

The woman catches me staring and excuses herself from the catering staff. She's wiping the corner of her mouth with a napkin as she rushes to me. "That goat cheese is delicious. Want to try some of the menu? We've got canapés, flambés, gazpacho..."

"No thank you. I was just running some errands for Mr. Keenly." I lift the box in my arms a little higher to prove it.

She takes it from me, placing it on a nearby bar. "Great. Thank you." She extends her arm out. "I'm Celia Owens, by the way. Mr. Keenly's assistant."

Say what?

I laugh. "Um...Olivia Margot." I return her handshake. "*Also* Keenly's assistant?"

Celia drops her arm. "Forgive me. That doesn't make much sense. I used to work for him. He called me last night saying it was an emergency and—"

"That I needed a competent assistant." Keenly walks into the ballroom taking short, hurried steps. He reminds me of a rodent, both in appearance and behavior.

I cross my arms in front of me wishing I could vanish. I don't know what the hell is going on, but it's clearly not going to look good for me.

Keenly joins us, holding his head high. "I had no choice but to hire you, Miss Margot. But I still needed a capable assistant, so I got Celia to come back and take care of things."

Come back? I can only imagine the reasons she would have left in the first place.

Celia plasters on a winning smile. "It's my pleasure to be helping the nation's best event planner."

"I knew you'd come around," Keenly says, rubbing Celia's shoulder. "Unfortunately, I can't just fire this one, but it's on the Stone's bill so I don't care what she does." He glares in my direction. "You can use her if you need any help." He lets out a boisterous guffaw as he says, "You'll be the assistant to the assistant. How will that look on your resumé?"

He scurries off before I can think of anything to say. I stare into the space he'd been occupying. What was I supposed to do now?

"Don't worry about him. He's an asshole."

I should learn that act she just put on for him. I'm not a fan of sucking up, but I also don't do well having enemies. Maybe because the only enemy I've ever had was myself.

Celia takes my arm and starts walking the perimeter of the room. "So, things I've learned over the years. Greg doesn't actually do all that much work. Most of this stuff, you schedule it, and it runs on autopilot. So what he delegates to me isn't all that much either. I basically get paid to do next to nothing. Which means for *you*, this is by far the best money you'll make for the least effort."

Great, so the easiest job also happens to be the most humiliating. "I'm not a fan of being useless."

"You won't be. Keenly, myself, and now you, we're just the eyes of the mission. And the mission is to make rich people feel even more important. So you supervise those who are working. Make sure they're doing what they're supposed to with a smile on their face."

We walk past men carrying white couches to the center of the room. By the big windows overlooking the coast, another group is piecing together a small wooden dance floor. On the other side of the room, a bar is being cleaned up and stocked with spotless glasses and liquor bottles. No one seems to be giving orders. Maybe Celia is right.

"There are other perks to this as well." She stops at a table and rummages through a small blue handbag. She brings out a wallet and plucks a card from it, handing it to me. "Business account. Now, you can't use it to buy a new car, but if it's related to work, it's covered by Platinum. So filling up your gas tank. Getting anything you need for Saturday. Hell, even after work drinks. Charge it, and consider it your bonus."

"You're serious? But then why did you stop working for them?"

"Isn't Keenly reason enough? There are only so many years one can handle working with that arrogant prick, but don't tell him I said so. He thinks I'm wasting my life, throwing it all away to start a family."

"He's a charmer." I like Celia. If she were running things, I'd feel more at ease with this job.

"Now, if you'll excuse me, I have to find a replacement bartender before Keenly realizes the old one quit."

She walks away before my brain catches up. *Maddie.* I spin around to chase after her. I have the perfect back up plan. She's fantastic and the guests will love her.

This is my opening to get Maddie into the party. After all she's done for me, this would be one way to pay her back.

Of course, in my sudden excitement, I forget my sub-par coordination in heels, shift my weight awkwardly onto one foot, twist my ankle, and tumble to the floor.

"Oh, honey! You okay?" Celia asks, rushing back.

That's one way to get her attention. *Focus, girl. Tell her about your wonderful best friend who'd be perfect for the job.*

"P-professional. Dedicated." Celia helps me up as I stutter nonsense.

She laughs. "Say that again."

I take a breath and pull my phone out, finding a photo of Maddie and hold it out for her.

Celia raises an eyebrow, waiting. A few chuckles from the catering table inform me I just had an audience.

I take a breath and force myself to create coherent sentences. I tell Celia about Maddie, sounding like I'm helping her campaign for presidency. But Celia nods, listening. She's way cooler than Keenly.

I expect her to ask more questions about her experience, but instead she says, "She's more graceful than you, correct?"

"Absolutely."

"Then bring her by on Thursday."

A goofy grin spreads across my face. I can't wait to tell her. I want to celebrate my mini-success. I just stepped up and got something done. Only a slight throb coming from my ankle reminds me how sloppy I was, but whatever. Celia's now my direct supervisor. I have a company credit card in my possession. And I just hooked my friend up with an unforgettable job. I'm on top of the damn world.

CHAPTER TEN

It's quiet at Brecken's Sports Pub. A couple sits quietly in a small booth staring at separate TV screens, seemingly unaware that they're here together. Two men sit on stools at the other end of the bar, and Maddie checks on them intermittently, returning to our conversation without missing a beat.

"So when's your first date?"

"Are you crazy? I barely got in two words with him. He was acting all weird, looking for something. Or someone..."

"You, maybe?" She leans in closer to me.

"I was standing right there, and it was like I was invisible." I fumble with my phone, checking the time every couple minutes. I should get home and try to unwind before tomorrow. These unpredictable days are going to get to me fast.

"So next time you're with him, pry a little further. You know he's got some sexy skeletons in his closet."

I believe his words to me were 'mind your own business'. I shake my head. "Not gonna happen."

The front door opens, and two more men walk through wearing suits, probably coming straight from work. Maddie flashes a bright smile at them, and both men seem to light up. This girl can accomplish more without a word, which reminds me I haven't told her she got a job.

She continues with her Devon spiel. "You know, you could find out some juicy information and then sell it to the tabloids. *ScandalLust* would flat out hire you, I bet."

"So which is it: date him or screw him over? I think he'd put a hit out for me if I got near the paparazzi."

Maddie had been on her way to her new customers, but she freezes mid-step. "Hold that thought." She grins, gets the guys' drink orders and returns. "A man unafraid to kill... That's a little sexy."

"And you're a little mental. No, I don't believe he's a murderer. At least, I don't think so. He's definitely hiding something though, and that's exactly what I don't want to get involved with."

"But you know you do. Mysterious. Gorgeous." She pulls her phone out from behind the bar to show me her newest wallpaper photo—a black-and-white Devon, shirtless, in jeans, looking extra angsty. "Lickable."

"Maddie!"

She fills two pint glasses from the tap as she bursts out laughing. "Relax. I put it on there this morning to mess with you. I knew you'd give me an open opportunity."

I hold onto her phone a minute longer while she takes the drinks over along with a plate of chips and salsa. Devon's icy gaze is penetrating, and the thought that this photo was taken for the general public... Well, what would it be like to be his girlfriend? What would I possibly learn about him that the whole world doesn't already know? How could I feel like I'm exclusively his when god knows how many other women gawk at photos just like this one?

Not to mention, he hardly knows I exist. Why bother imagining life as his girlfriend, when I don't even register on his list of things worth paying attention to? It's pointless.

Maddie snatches the phone out from under me. "You're overthinking things. I can sense it."

"Yeah, well, you can use those same psychic abilities in a couple days when you meet him."

She's half-listening as she works—pouring colorful bottles of liquor and juice into a shaker filled with ice. She finishes making a tropical martini and places it in front of me. She considers what I just said and laughs. "What? You dragging him to the apartment or something?"

"You're running the bar at the party Saturday. I'm bringing you by to meet Celia on Thursday, and fortunately for us both, she's much nicer than that Keenly asshole."

She hesitates as if trying to gauge whether or not this is payback for the Devon photo on her phone. "You're serious?"

"You know I'm never funny when I try." I take a sip from my drink. Images of the beach and Devon flash across my mind. As good as this tastes—tangy and sweet—I can only imagine what he tastes like...

"You *are* serious. Oh my god! I could kiss you right now." She lunges across the counter and kisses my cheek with an exaggerated and loud *muah*. "You're the most amazing woman on the planet Olivia Margot."

By now all six patrons are staring in our direction. Their curious eyes linger for an uncomfortable moment before they return to their respective staring and drinking.

Maddie settles down and leans in to talk quieter. "So you got Devon to get me a job too? You're on a roll."

"No, I talked to Celia directly. Why would I tell Devon about you? He'd ditch me in a heartbeat."

"Oh please." She turns her back to type things into a computer. Receipts print out, she takes them to their owners, and she comes back. "You have no idea how much I owe you for this. That drink is totally on the house." Her eyes brighten. "Better yet, I'm going to help you get Devon Stone."

One look at her, and I know she's committed. This was supposed to be my favor to her, and having her at the party was supposed to make it easier on me. But now with Maddie plotting some sort of game plan... Now I didn't know what to expect.

She wanders off to collect credit cards and empty glasses. I gulp my martini faster.

CHAPTER ELEVEN

I can hear Celia talking to decorators when I arrive the next morning. My aching feet follow her voice, and I curse myself for wearing heels yesterday. And for what reason? To impress a guy? That worked out well.

I find Celia in the ballroom where people are installing extravagant light fixtures and hanging elegant tapestries from the walls to block off extra doors and entryways. The couches I saw yesterday are set up in a casual cluster in the center of the ballroom providing a comfortable lounge amongst the formal tables, and the big glass doors leading to the back patio are wide open, inviting in a refreshing ocean breeze that dances amongst all the fabric. The same linens I dropped off to be dry-cleaned yesterday are being unwrapped from their protective plastic and draped over the tables. It's good to know I didn't mess up that task, and now I can see the room coming together—white and cream and full of class. I'm impressed.

"Keenly hasn't been by yet," Celia says as if we were in mid-conversation. "But feel free to stick around. I'm assuming he'll have some sort of to-do list when he gets here, and we can split it and probably end our work day quicker." She smiles and turns to adjust the positioning of a smaller side table.

I feel awkward standing around while productivity happens around me, so I hobble out the doors into the fresh air. This way, I should see Keenly coming and can jump right back into the action. I've never felt more inadequate.

Sunlight glistens off the surface of the pool, mimicking the same sparkling of the ocean itself. Forget the chairs. I sit down in a spot near the pool where it looks like the water flows right into the Pacific. Stretching out my aching legs, I close my eyes and take in the invigorating breeze. This place is heaven.

"Is this you working again?"

I snap my head up and see Devon leaning against the railing of the nearest balcony. His car wasn't out front. Where'd he come from?

"I'm waiting," I call back. Reaching into my purse, I pull out my phone, needing something to make me appear busy. I'm not going to play the role of the idle dummy again today. I disregard Devon, since he'll disappear in a second anyway, and instead, turn on my phone to find a missed text from Maddie:

Is he there? Tell me he is!

I smile and send her back a little thumbs-up icon.

From the corner of my eye, I see Devon walk down a set of steps, coming toward me. What does he want now?

He stops next to me and sits down just as casually as I had minutes ago. "You trying to ignore me today?"

He's wearing raggedy jeans again—maybe the same ones from yesterday—a black v-neck undershirt and flip-flops. This jerk can even make flip-flops look sexy. I have to remind myself not to stare at him.

"Not ignoring you. Just here to work." My phone buzzes, and I look down to see Maddie's sent me a response:

Get me more info on his hot brother.

She's included a photo of Devon and Kaidan standing together on the red carpet. I angle my phone so he can't see the screen.

"So...Olivia." Hearing him say my name catches my attention. *He does remember.* "How'd you end up in party planning?"

He looks down at me and shifts in his spot. His leg is almost grazing mine, and I find myself staring at the torn knee of his jeans. Something as stupidly ordinary as a few inches of tan skin leaves me entranced, and the heat from his closeness rises up like a growing wildfire, spreading up my legs, settling in the core of my body. I focus on keeping my breath steady, and my phone goes off again:

Seriously girl. Ask what's in those genes.

Another buzz:

Better yet, ask what's in those jeans ;-)

I feel my cheeks flush as I slam my finger against the button to shut off my phone and jam it back into my purse. "Sorry. I...um...went to school. For hospitality. I haven't found a career yet. As you can probably tell. But... yeah. So I'm just here for now."

I adjust myself to add a couple inches between us. He's acting vaguely interested in my stammering, so I need to get it together— and fast. I move my feet to position them on one side of me and wince from the brief pain that leaves me wondering how runway models can handle stilettos but I can't last a day in three-inch pumps.

"You okay?" Devon asks.

Not really. You're being too friendly, and I can't figure out your motives.

"Yeah, it's just my feet. They're sore from yesterday." I laugh at myself. "But I don't know why I'm telling you that. So you tell me. What do you do when you aren't busy being rich and famous?"

He gives me one of his irresistible grins and answers while reaching over and grabbing ahold of my feet. Before I can stop him, he swivels my legs back around, placing them on his lap. I might have a heart attack.

"My time is spent helping pretty women get jobs and dodging any further questions about my personal life."

He unstraps my sandals, removing each one slowly. He called me pretty. He's touching me. My legs are the luckiest legs in all of L.A., and I can't stop thinking about how we're one thin layer of denim and a quiet room away from being two longtime lovers recovering after an intense horizontal workout.

The cold water from the pool lurches me back to reality as Devon drops my feet into it with a splash. I shriek with surprise but immediately realize the throbbing in my feet is subsiding, and my shock turns into giggles. "You did not just do that!"

He smiles back. "I figured that would help. Here, so you don't feel as ridiculous."

Devon places his flip-flops next to my sandals and hitches up the legs of his jeans. Ladies and gentlemen, we have calves—muscular, tanned calves.

He plunges his own feet in, and now his wet, left leg is right up against my right. I'm trying to keep from running my toes along his ankle, but it's tempting.

Devon leans back with his arms outstretched to hold his weight. A cruel move as his muscles tense, stretching out the sleeve of his shirt.

"So..." I need a distraction. "I—uh—got my friend Maddie a job working the party too. She's my roommate and really great. Pretty. Smart."

"I'm just going to stop you there."

I clamp my mouth shut. What did I do?

"I was asking about you," he says with this casual tone. His directness sends a shiver up my arms and through my chest. "Come here."

Where? I'm already here. He sits up straighter, puts his arm around me, and pulls me in closer. This is the best invitation I've ever received. Even better than that one time in fourth grade when Cara Summers—the coolest girl in my class—asked me to come to her Spring Break sleepover. Granted, as much as I felt out of place back then—with all the fancy, preteen magazines and my lack of co-ordination with a hair curler—it was nothing compared to the out-of-body experience I am currently having.

I swear I'm melting under his touch, but I refuse to move. Number Three has pulled me into his grasp. He can keep me forever. This close to him, even his scent has me drunk with lust. I'm almost paralyzed.

He gives me a little shake. "Oh, Olivia. If we're going to be friends, you're going to have to open up..."

Open what?

"But it's all right. You working here, and us seeing each other, you'll loosen right up to my charming ways."

I'm sure I will...

But—"Why are you being nice to me now?" I ask. He has to be up to something.

"Oh right. I've been kind of a dick, haven't I?"

"Kind of." I slap a hand over my mouth. "Sorry."

He lets out a laugh, a real live laugh. "She speaks the truth. I can appreciate that. And I'm sorry. My mind's been elsewhere. I've been trying to..." He trails off, distracting me by sliding his foot under mine, leaving my leg to rest right on top of his.

What had he been saying? Oh right. "Trying to what? You've been acting strange."

He almost cuts me off again. "Don't worry about it. Tell me where you grew up."

I've never experienced so many mixed signals before. His leg touching mine. His sudden interest in us being friends. His refusal to talk about himself. And his blunt rudeness when I ask him anything. I'm being yanked around like a tug-o-war rope.

"I... I grew up here." I say, wanting to keep the conversation going but unsure what to make of Devon's behavior.

"Right in my backyard? See, you are full of surprises."

I laugh out loud, grateful for the ease that washes over me. So what if he doesn't want to tell me his life story? Why would he? And the longer it takes for him to open up to me, the more time I get to spend with him. I can't complain about that.

"I was born and raised here—in California." I giggle again. *Keep yourself under con-*

trol. "We moved a bit. But I came here after for college and didn't leave."

"UCLA?"

"Cal State."

He nods quietly. It's my turn to ask him something, so I say the first thing that comes to mind. "So what's it like being a twin?" Ugh. How lame.

"I don't want to talk about my brother. What about you? Family? Siblings?"

"I don't want to talk about my brother either."

He smiles. "Glad to see we have something in common."

I doubt that. But I'm not about to explain why he's wrong. I can feel myself closing up again. Fortunately, an angry stomping approaches from behind.

"Miss. Margot." Keenly spits out each word with revulsion. "What in the name of professionalism is going on here?"

CHAPTER TWELVE

I yank my feet out of the water and hurry to get upright. I stick a slippery foot into each sandal, and lean down to strap them, ignoring the spongy feel of the wet soles. Snatching my purse still lying on the ground, I'm certain I look like an ass to my boss right now.

"Sorry. Mr. Keenly. I was just waiting on you. Celia said—"

"Celia said to take a dip in the pool?"

"Of course not. That was my choice." Well, Devon's choice. He's standing behind me now, and I'm fully aware he's close. So close that if I leaned back, even slightly, I'd be resting against his chest. My heart flutters, and I blush. But I am here to work... "Is there anything I can do for you today, Mr. Keenly?"

He flares his nostrils as if just now noticing an awful smell. "You know? You can. Go to Exotic Blooms on Santa Monica. See their floral arrangements. Send me photos. And I'll tell you which will be used for the party."

Couldn't he have the florist send the photos themselves? "No problem." Anything to get away from him. "Is there something you want specifically?"

"Yes. For you to not make a single decision. No matter what, you are to call me. I can imagine the sort of things you'd approve. And if you'd like to keep your job, I suggest you not bother my friend Devon here."

"Friend, my ass." Devon steps forward. "And the only one bothering me right now is you."

"Then forgive me, but Miss Margot has work to do. Even if she wasn't bothering you, she should have been inside—"

"I was helping her. And you shouldn't be so presumptuous."

"Helping her do what, Mr. Stone?" Keenly glances at me and back at Devon. I'm just going to stand here and play along with whatever Devon wants to say.

"Go to the florist, clearly." He turns to me. "You ready?"

Just smile and nod. "Yep."

We stride past Keenly, and I feel like we're two teenagers making our getaway from a disapproving teacher. I stop by my car and turn back toward him. "Thank you. I don't know why he hates me."

"He hates most people. But then again, most people hate him back. It's the paying clients that adore him. He puts on a hell of a facade for them."

I smile, and pull out my phone to look up the address for Exotic Blooms.

"I meant it when I said I'd help."

I eye him suspiciously. It's one thing to make small talk in the backyard, but if he really wants to go with me to run an errand... something's going on. "No thanks. You don't have to." I find the address and open my car door.

"Oh, so you've got this now? I should just run along?"

I turn around to see him waiting there, a condescending look on his face.

"What? You *want* to go with me? Am I supposed to believe that?"

At what point should I call him out on his bullshit? I'd give anything to be able to read his mind and know what he's up to right now.

"Isn't it funny how Exotic Blooms sounds more like a gentlemen's club than a flower shop?"

"Sure. Funny." I check the time and consider getting into the car and leaving, letting Devon hang in mid-thought.

"It's because it is."

"Is what?"

"A strip club." He snatches my phone and messes with my maps application.

"I just got the address for it. It's a flower shop. Don't mess up my directions."

"There's a florist of the same name on the same street. And see..." He hands the phone back to me. He'd gone into the address' details and scrolled down to Exotic Blooms' official website. "Go ahead. Tap the link."

I do, and I'm immediately greeted with a window asking me to validate I'm over the age of eighteen.

Devon continues, knowing he's right. "If you'd gone to the address you'd selected, you'd have gotten there during their midday happy hour. That one's the strip club, not the florist. Funny, I've made the opposite mistake before."

It takes a second for the meaning of that to dawn on me. Gross. "Lovely."

"I'm glad I could help. Now let me call my driver and be sure you get to the right location in style."

His driver? I guess that explains why his car is nowhere in sight.

"Don't you think it goes against employer-employee appropriateness?" I say, because it's beyond unacceptable to be hanging out with the indirect boss of my boss.

Devon pulls out his own phone and hits a few soundless buttons. "I'm a firm believer in being inappropriate. But I'm not your employer."

"I do take this job seriously, you know? I need it. And I can't have Mr. Keenly thinking I don't—"

He holds his free hand up to protest. "Hey. I'm only assisting you in being more productive. I assure you, my driver takes his job seriously too. Accept the ride—my friendly offer to you—and you'll be on your way to being the most efficient party planner in all the U.S."

As if by cue, a dark gray Mercedes-Benz pulls around the corner and stops in front of us. The windows are so dark, it's hard to see the person behind the wheel, but a second later, the driver's side door opens, and a man in a black suit hops out. Devon gives him a subtle wave, like a secret hand signal, and the man retreats back into the car.

Devon walks to the rear passenger door and opens it. "So?" He looks at me. "What are you waiting for?"

"Fine. Okay. Thank you." I shut my own car door and approach him. "But what's the catch?"

"No catch." He adds in an innocent, puppy dog face. "I'm here to help."

"Mhmm." I step past him and climb into the backseat.

The driver turns and reaches his hand back to shake mine. "I'm Mark. Where're we headed?"

"Olivia," I say, returning the handshake. "And Exotic Blooms—the florist." I add the extra emphasis and hear Devon chuckle from outside.

Mark nods and turns back around. This *will* be easier. No getting lost. No ending up at a completely different and uncomfortable location. But Devon still waits by the open door. What should I say to him? *I know you're up to something, so you can just wait here until I get back?*

I can't even make eye contact without smiling though. "What?" I ask him, not bothering to hide my improving mood.

"I mean," he starts. "I'd hate for you to be lonely in that seat. All by yourself. No one to talk to."

"I can talk to Mark."

"Sorry ma'am," Mark interjects. "Mr. Stone has a strict no-talking-while-driving rule."

"You're making that up," I say to him and then turn to Devon. "He's making that up."

I know he's holding out until he hears exactly what he wants. With that mystery and intrigue mixed with stubborn sexiness, I can't imagine anyone being able to tell him no.

"Fine." I sigh and scoot over. "Let's go. I hope you're bored out of your mind."

"Nothing's boring with me," he says, sliding into the seat next to me.

And I believe him.

CHAPTER THIRTEEN

It's only when we're in the closed confines of the backseat that I notice my pulse quickening. It was one thing talking to him in the open space of the patio. I felt relaxed and was more curious by his random moment of interest in me to even second-guess what I was doing. But in here, aside from Mark, I feel like we're somewhere private. My mind is a mush of thoughts.

He's so close. I want to touch him. The heat from being outside has given his skin a light sheen of sweat. He'd be salty to the taste. I *want* to taste him.

I force myself to turn back toward the window while I steady my breathing.

We're passing the gates when he speaks. "Look at me."

An order.

One of his hands finds my chin, making me turn in his direction. What does he want? Is he going to kiss me? Maybe I should let him. Wait, why would he do that? We don't even know each other. But then, why would he—

"If you're gawking out the window, the pap assholes will get you in a shot. Unless you want to be plastered in a tabloid..."

Oh. So he's being helpful again.

He drops his hand, and I feel my cheeks warm realizing all my instant assumptions were way off base. "Thanks," I say, meekly.

"You fascinate me, you know."

"What, like a sideshow?" Are the ratty jeans and tee his way of mocking me? I know I'm not rich and glamorous, but I'm put together decently. He smiles, and I know that's not at all what he meant.

"The exact opposite." He looks out toward the passing buildings and the beach beyond them. "It's funny. I'd almost believe you really don't know who I am. The way you act...you're not like most girls I come across."

Because I *don't* know him. Other than what I saw online and the whole "Lust List" thing. Number Three, I remind myself. But I can't let him know that. Then I would be exactly like those girls he's talking about. I decide to challenge him instead. "How do you expect me to know you, when you haven't told me anything about yourself?"

He waits a long moment before answering, and I wonder if he's just going to redirect our conversation again.

"I have a father and a brother—both of whom have their heads shoved up their asses.

This party you're throwing? It's for my dad to announce his retirement—as though it's a surprise for anyone. The even bigger non-surprise is he's giving Kaidan everything, the entire company."

"And you want it?"

"Hell no. But even if I did, they wrote me off a long time ago."

"Why?" Maybe Devon Stone doesn't always get what he wants. It's not the label he cares about though. The tone in his voice makes it clear there's more to it than business.

"I never kissed their asses. I didn't care about the fame or the money. Even with its perks, it comes with more than that. That's what people don't realize. You're a celebrity? Great. Here's a one-way ticket to bad decisions and addictions and an all out rampage on your psychological well-being. People use you. They stick you up on this pedestal and expect you to be a god. But then they exploit you and make up all sorts of shit to make you look like trash." He runs a hand through his hair as he continues. I'm baffled by how extraordinarily normal he seems right now. I did automatically assume he was privileged and lucky. That he got whatever he wanted and never had to worry about anything. The reality made him seem almost...ordinary, making me feel bad for him. "So while the wonderful Kaidan continues to honor the family legacy, Devon Stone is the officially-licensed punching bag of the Stone Empire."

Wow. "I don't know what to say. That's... I mean, how could they do that to you?"

He laughs. "Don't get me wrong. I did my share to earn my reputation, but they just made it easier to give in to *the dark side*."

I smile though I don't believe for one second that all this doesn't hurt him deeper than his 'bad boy' exterior. "So then why do you hang around there? You should get on with your own life and cut them loose."

"I have business to attend to right now. Suspicions I need to clarify. You've caught me at an odd time. Usually, I don't step foot near that house."

"So where do you live?"

Devon reaches over and pushes a loose strand of hair behind my ear. "That's top secret information." He gives me that grin that makes me dissolve into a flutter of nerves, and before I can ask anything else, we pull into a parking lot and come to a stop.

Devon hops out of the SUV to open my door like a perfect gentleman, and I step out smoothing out my shirt. My mind is reeling from the amount of information I just got from him. As sexy as "Lust List" Devon is, this new version—Sincere Devon—is irresistibly alluring. It's like we're two, normal people facing our own collection of demons.

Another car pulls into a space near us as I grab my purse.

There's a quiet pause after Devon closes the door, and then *click.*

"Fuck." Devon takes my hand and pulls me inside the shop in a rush. He yanks the door closed and reaches up to twist the lock. "Sorry. They're everywhere."

So much for ordinary.

Two paparazzi climb out of the car, still snapping away as a second car pulls in, not bothering to park in a designated spot.

"Are these the same people from the mansion?" I ask, attempting to cover my face with my purse.

"Around here, who knows? There are so many of them, don't bother trying to tell them apart."

I try to put distance between me and the shop windows where three camera lenses are pressed against the glass. I'm sick to my stomach knowing Devon has to deal with this frequently. Having unwanted pictures taken of him and then plastered all over. I'm lucky to be out of the spotlight.

But I'm not. They're clearly taking photos of both of us. I can't help but glance back. *Click. Click.* Still there and aiming right at me.

"How do I make them stop?" I don't want them here. It's horrifying. Violating. And there's no way I'm leaving this store until they go away.

"There is no making them stop." Devon eyes me carefully. "Are you okay?"

No. The constant clicking. The forced attention. It reminds me of something else...

News crews. Waiting outside of my parent's house.

I hid up in my room for over a week, knowing if I tried to leave the house they'd be out there with their questions. *"How are you handling the tragic loss of your only brother?"*

"When do you plan to return to school?"

"How does it feel knowing the alleged murderers walked the same halls, shared the same teachers? Same classes?"

I blink back tears and steady my breathing hoping Devon isn't paying that much attention. "I'm fine. Let's just..." I walk to the counter where the florist is waiting, hardly fazed by the fiasco outside.

The sweet-looking, older woman brings out samples of centerpieces, and they're all larger than life and gorgeous. Enormous bunches of white and cream roses and lilies and hydrangeas. I'm in awe of the last one on the end. Orchids.

I'm drawn to them like a magnet. "These have always been my favorite," I tell no one in particular. "Each one is so extraordinary it stands beautifully all by itself."

I'm admiring the natural splendor when my phone begins to ring. It's Keenly, and he repeats what he said before. I'm not to make any decisions. So I hang up, take a photo of the flowers to send to him, and he tells me to order the roses.

I relay this information to the florist. "He wants twenty of the full centerpieces and eight hundred extra stems—half cream and half white—of the—"

"Orchids," Devon finishes. "All white. However many you have, and make them look

as good as that." He points to the arrange-
ment.

"No, Mr. Keenly said—"

"I don't care what he said. Those orchids
are perfect. Each one, all on its own. It
doesn't need a bunch of other pretty flowers
to be stunning." He's staring straight at me,
not looking at a single flower. "It just stands
on its own in sheer beauty." He turns back to
the florist while my heart flutters. "Also, I'm
the boss. I can override his requests. It gives
me great pleasure to do so." He adds a wink in
my direction that's either to confirm his ha-
tred for Keenly or to flirt with me further. I
have no idea. I'm far from in control here.
Every cell in my body is fighting the urge to
flee and return to normal life—whatever
normal is. I can't remember right now.

We finish ordering and get ready to leave.
I hesitate and Devon notices. "Come on. It's
okay."

He wraps an arm around me and makes for
the door with his usual confidence and sense

of authority. He pushes it open with enough force that the paparazzi waiting jump back and make space for us. I notice none of them get close enough to make physical contact.

I keep myself focused on the car, getting in as fast as I can, and when I'm safely behind the tinted glass, my mind wanders to what just happened in the store. Devon was just being nice, right? He knew I was uncomfortable, so he did something kind to distract me. He hates Keenly and resents his family, so of course, he'd go out of his way to be passive aggressive.

Devon opens his door, and I can hear he's yelling at one of the camera guys. "...Like last time. You understand, dickhead?"

He climbs in and slams the door shut. The *clicking* of shutters continues as we pull away. Then they rush back to their vehicles and race to catch up. I slouch down in my seat not wanting them to see even the top of my head.

"You can just ignore them now," he says, as if reading my mind.

How can he just forget about them so easily? They're following us. "I'm surprised they don't get all in your face. I suppose there's some humanity in them."

"That's not them being polite. I've punched one too many. They know I don't play games."

Oh. "So you just...hit them?" It's almost comical.

He doesn't laugh. "Sure. I just hit them. Then I *just* got arrested. And then just had to do community service. And just had to deal with the aftermath from my father. And every moment was just covered in the same trashy tabloids those assholes sell their photos to, beginning the circle again."

It's not so comical anymore.

"You've truly never been involved with any of this before?" He smiles. "I think my first baby photos were even taken by them."

I shake my head. "I have no idea how you live the way you do. I'm not sure I'd want to if I had the choice."

"At least you'd have the choice."

He reaches over and lifts my chin to meet his gaze again. His hand, so soft yet powerful, matches the look in his eyes, and I can feel the heat radiating between us. "I like that about you."

"Like what?"

"I know you're not into all this. Yet, you're curious what it would be like if this were your life."

Sure. What would it be like to date him? Are celebrities even the dinner-and-a-movie type of people? I highly doubt that. But I'm not the type of person who will find out. Even the fantasy of it all is too much.

"I'm not curious. I'm perfectly content with my own..." I trail off, knowing whatever I said next would be a lie.

And then Devon leans in, and his lips meet mine. My breath catches in my throat, and I give in to his kiss. Never mind, I *am* curious. I want to be a part of his life. I don't care what goes with it. The cameras and the chaos. I'll deal with it all if I can have this.

...If I can have him.

Devon Stone kisses with a sense of mischief. His warm lips graze mine slowly at first. But then he doesn't hesitate to add enough force to pull my mouth open and tease me with his tongue. Running it along my upper lip, he brings all my senses to life. Then he crushes his mouth against mine, kissing me with urgency, only to pull away and leave me wanting more. So much more.

I'm breathless and can't think straight. What was that? Why? He could have any other girl, yet after three days of his strange behavior with me, he proves he's even more unpredictable.

"Mark. Take us to the docks, buddy." He turns to me, his fingers tracing a circle on my knee. "I'll take you somewhere special."

Okay. I don't even care to ask where. I'd go anywhere with him.

Holy shit. I'd go anywhere with him.

I feel myself stiffen from that terrifying realization. No. That's not an option. I have to speak up. "I can't," I blurt out. "Sorry. I'm working. I need to get back, and..."

"And let your boss treat you like dirt some more? It's just one afternoon. You can work later."

"No. Devon. I...just. No." I speak up for Mark. "I have to head back, but thank you." He nods but returns to ignoring his passengers.

Devon leans back in his seat. "Olivia. Come on. It's not a big deal—"

"It is. I have a job. I'm on the clock." And I'm your employee. A middle-class worker. Not some rock star, supermodel. "Listen, I don't know what you want from me." I was right. He did have a motive. "I could tell you were up to something when—"

"Up to what? We hung out. Things were fine. You—"

"What about yesterday, when you barely knew my name? Or the day before when you blew me off? Or the day before that, when—oh that's right, you didn't even know I existed. So you're suddenly nice to me now? You go with me to order flowers for a party you don't care about. You *kiss* me? And I'm supposed to believe you have no intentions here?"

"Right. Because I can't just be a nice guy getting to know a nice girl?"

He admitted his own violent streak. He's been arrested. He's got an entire history of *not* being a nice guy. "I don't know what to think Devon. We don't know each other. I'm not going to ditch my job—which is important to me—to do whatever it is you expect me to do with you." No matter how much I want to.

"You think I wanted to take you somewhere to fuck? Is that it?"

"Am I that far off after the open invitation you gave me two days ago?"

He laughs and shakes his head. "Maybe I had it wrong. Maybe you aren't much different from others."

"Don't say that. You don't know me—"

"And you're not giving me much of a chance to." He's starting to raise his voice.

"Was that part of the job description I missed—set aside time for Devon to get to know the assistant to the assistant? I don't recall seeing that on Mr. Keenly's to-do lists yet, so sorry. I haven't given you a chance to know me when you had zero interest yesterday."

I shift in the seat so I can look out my window instead. What did he want from me? Suddenly we're friends? Suddenly we're more than that? What did I miss, and how the hell am I the bad guy for being responsible?

We ride the rest of the way in silence, the heat between us long gone and replaced with suffocating tension. When we get back to the house, Devon doesn't bother to play the gentleman role anymore, and instead, marches toward the back of the house as I make my way to the front doors. I hesitate on the steps trying to remember why I'm here. *It's a job. Just a job.*

I go inside knowing that the wrath of Keenly is now nothing compared to whatever just happened between me and Devon.

CHAPTER FOURTEEN

I didn't warn Maddie about the spectacle she'd be walking into when she got home. I can't stop thinking about Devon. I don't know if I'm more angry or enamored. I'm pissed off from our argument and how he just disappeared after. But something happened today. He opened up to me, and he didn't have to. He went out of his way to defend me in front of Keenly and then accompany me on a mindless errand. And he didn't have to. I'm not an idiot. There's something going on.

And I have to figure out how to put a stop to it. For all I know, he's done with me, but I need to convince myself I'm not interested in him at all. Unfortunately, I'm an awful liar, especially with myself.

So here's the sight Maddie sees when she gets home. Her pitiful roommate is lying on the couch staring at the TV that's not only off, it's unplugged too. But I hadn't stopped there. Before falling into a comatose state on the couch, I disconnected the Internet, hid my laptop and cell phone in Maddie's room, and I shoved the love seat in front of her door.

"What's going on here?" Maddie asks slowly, taking in the scene.

I knew if I gave in, I'd spend hours obsessing over every article, gawking at every publicized photo, and overanalyzing every little thing that's happened over the past couple days. Like any rational person would do, I removed all methods of research, leaving only my mind to relive today over and over. "He kissed me."

"Whoa. What?" She drops her purse on the love seat blocking off her door, and sinks down into the cushion next to it, hardly caring that I've rearranged our living space and locked her out of her room. "Spill, woman."

"I went to work. He talked to me. He kissed me. We argued. I blew it." That sums it up.

Maddie shakes her head. "But yesterday..."

"Yesterday, he didn't know who I was. Yeah, I addressed that in our argument. Didn't seem to help my case."

"What did you fight about?"

She sounds more impressed than surprised. Of course she would. I haven't put myself in a situation to have guy trouble in over a year, and suddenly here I am, skipping the drawn out, stressful relationship, and diving head first into the "we need to talk" stage.

"I...um...I guess I accused him of wanting to sleep with me."

"But he did, didn't he?"

"Which is why I accused him. But Number Three does not like to be questioned." I laugh and throw a couch pillow over my face. "I don't know what I'm doing Maddie," I scream into the pillow.

"I'm not sure I know either. But I don't think disconnecting from all of technology is going to solve your problems."

I sit up and look at her. "Sorry. It's just...he kissed me. And. Wow. It should be illegal to kiss like that because I was tempted to do whatever he wanted, and he wanted me to blow off my job to go with him."

"To have sex?"

"Apparently not. But I didn't get a chance to find out. He's mad now. I'm mad now. Who does he think he is trying to get me to skip work, like my financial well-being doesn't matter?"

"A rich guy who doesn't have to worry about that." She keeps a straight face for a second before we both burst into a fit of giggles.

"I would've been much better off getting a job at some Waffle House or something."

"Much better off and so, *so* bored." She stands up and escapes to the kitchen, coming back a moment later with two beers and her eyes glued to her phone. "Drink this."

I accept the bottle and take a sip. "Thanks. But this isn't going to solve anything either."

"No, but you'll want it when you see this." She's still staring at her phone as she reads, "'Roses Are Red and So's Devon's Blushing Brunette.'"

My stomach seems to do a somersault as my mind pieces together what I'm about to see.

Maddie keeps reading. "'Devon Stone was seen today with an unknown woman as they ran a suburban errand at Exotic Blooms. Stone is better suited for the alternative location, but while there were no naked ladies in this flower shop, who knows what he's being treated to tonight.'" I snatch the phone out of her hands to see it for myself. "What are they talking about? This nonsense is passed off as journalism now?"

I'm not listening to Maddie as I see my first tabloid appearance. They used a shot of us leaving the store. Devon's arm around me while I look horrified and awkward and embarrassed. Great. I guess it could be worse. At least I'm not scratching my nose or tripping on the sidewalk, but seeing us together in a photo—how could we ever be a match? It's all too obvious that on the ladder of importance and belonging, Devon's on top and I'm... across the street as the quiet observer.

"You two are hot together." Maddie sits next to me looking at the photo again. "He's all close to you like he really likes you, and—"

"Is this supposed to make me feel better?" I hold up the phone. "It all went downhill from here. I doubt he'd come this close again."

Maddie lays her head on my shoulder. "There you go, making assumptions about him again. Just wait until tomorrow before you go writing this one off."

CHAPTER FIFTEEN

I probably would have called in sick this morning if it weren't Thursday. But I have to take Maddie with me, so there's no way I'd get out of going to the Stone mansion today. Instead, I'm counting on Devon being mad enough to not show up.

We pull up to the mansion, and Maddie is just as wide-eyed as I was when I first saw the place. "Wow. What are my chances of scoring the other brother?"

I park the car and glare at her. "You're here to work. Take it seriously, please."

She straightens her face into a stern look. "Yes, ma'am. Very serious."

My phone buzzes with the 10:00 am alarm. Good timing. "Let's go."

I lead her in through the front door, and all is quiet inside. Assuming everyone is in the back ballroom, we walk through the house, stopping every several feet while Maddie is taken aback by the luxury of it all.

"A little different than our apartment, huh?" I say.

"You're telling me."

We walk past the kitchen where she freezes again. Devon's in there. Time seems to stop as I see an identical replica of the first Lust List photo I saw of him. He's leaning against the kitchen counter, casually eating an apple. Lucky apple. He's wearing a black button-down shirt—currently unbuttoned—and cargo shorts. I never thought someone could carelessly look this good.

"Good morning ladies." He smiles that millionaire grin of his.

"Oh good god," Maddie mumbles next to me.

I elbow her to snap her out of it. "Keep walking." Devon holds my gaze for a moment longer before I break away and head toward the ballroom.

Amidst all the party preparations, I spot Celia talking to Keenly. The room is almost ready for Saturday. I'm not sure what more work can be done, but I'm certain Mr. Keenly would think otherwise. He sees me walking over, says something quietly to Celia, and rushes away.

After introducing Maddie to Celia, I turn to find Devon standing behind me.

"You know, you'll break my fragile little ego if you try to avoid me."

"I highly doubt that." I notice Maddie is turned away from Celia and gawking at Devon. "Maddie, Devon. Devon, Maddie."

"Hey," she says, keeping it unnaturally cool. I almost laugh seeing Maddie Lowell—

for the first time ever—try to keep control of herself. "Nice place you got here."

"It's not my place." He doesn't even look in her direction, and instead stares at me. "Can we talk?"

Did that just happen? My super gorgeous roommate just tried to get his attention and he ignored her the same way he ignored me the other day?

I turn to Maddie and spin her back to Celia. "Get to work." I look to Celia, "Do you need anything from me right now?"

She tries to hide a knowing smile. "Nah. We're fine in here."

I reluctantly follow Devon out of the room. We end up in the study at the front of the house—the same one Devon and his father argued in during my interview. This room matches the office across the foyer, only instead of a desk, there are couches and a coffee table. I settle into a leather chair, dropping my purse between my feet, and try to think of what I should say. I'm still not sure what I did wrong, but I feel like I owe him an apology.

"I'm sorry," Devon says before I can say it myself.

"Me too."

He walks along the perimeter of the room, eyeing the walls of bookshelves. "You don't need to apologize. I was being a jerk. I shouldn't pull you away from your work."

Like you are right now? "No, you shouldn't."

"And I shouldn't throw last minute surprises at you. It seems like you don't do well with them."

"No, I don't."

Devon stops at a shelf focusing on a small box sitting on it. He opens it and shifts things around inside. Seeming disappointed, he closes it and continues walking. Again with the ulterior motives. What is he doing?

"I have a boat."

He makes me want to scream. He rarely makes sense, and when he does, *I'm* the one who misinterprets him. "And?"

"That's where I was going to take you yesterday." On the opposite side of the room from me, he stoops down and attempts to open a locked set of doors. He stands up abruptly and pulls a set of keys from his pocket. His attention is so far from me as he returns to those doors, trying out one key at a time.

"Can you just stop?" I say, raising my voice.

Taken by surprise, he whips back around.

"I don't know what you're doing," I say as he follows my gaze back to the locked doors. "Or why. But just stop and talk to me for a second without having other, more important things on your mind. Talk *to me*."

He stands up and leans against the shelves. "We have a family yacht. It's available to all of us, anytime we want. I was going to bring you on it. Give you an afternoon to relax. Nothing else."

That wasn't what I'd expected. "Thanks. I guess. But—"

"You can go with me this afternoon. I'm meeting some friends on it, so it may not be as quiet as it would've been yesterday. But maybe that'll make you more comfortable. A group instead of just the two of us."

Just the two of us. I like the sound of that. But no, I'm not being pushed around anymore.

"Tell me what you're doing first."

"I just said, we're going on the boat."

"No. I mean right now. You expect me to go out on the ocean with you, yet I've been watching you play cat burglar all week. You're looking for something. And you said you think your family has screwed you over. What is it?"

He studies the little locked doors again. "My father's will. I think he wrote me out."

"Why don't you just ask him?"

"I did. He told me to drop it."

Funny, I know how that one feels. "So you're trying to find it anyway?"

"I am."

"Is it in here?"

"I've searched everywhere else. He doesn't use this room much, but I suppose that makes it a good hiding place."

"But you have keys..."

"That I've spent this week finding and copying."

That makes a little more sense. "So? Go ahead." This isn't my family drama, and that makes it a little exciting. It's like we're having a Bonnie and Clyde moment, and I'm loving the trust he just put in me.

Devon tries a couple more keys before the door swings open. Inside is a safe. "Dammit," he says. But then he starts hitting buttons, trying code after code. Something tells me he's been snooping around his family for years. A long beep indicates he finally entered the right combination, and he hurries to go through the contents inside. "Yes!" He looks back at me. "You must be my lucky charm. I've been trying to get this thing for weeks."

He pulls out a sealed envelope and locks everything back up.

"Won't he notice it's gone?"

"Not in the time it takes me to make copies and return it." He stands upright right as we hear footsteps coming from outside. "Shit."

He rushes over to me, kneels down, and shoves the envelope into my bag as the door to the study opens.

I hear a man clear his throat and realize without context, it's just Devon hanging out between my legs with a slight look of panic on both our faces. My reputation in this house is getting better by the day...

In the doorway, Calvin Stone gives his son a cold stare. "I want to speak to you."

"Sure," Devon says. He pulls the zipper of my purse closed and gives me a knowing stare before following his father out.

I'm officially an accomplice.

Out in the ballroom, Maddie is pouring a variety of colorful drinks for Celia, showing off her skills. I join them at the bar where they both eye me with anticipation.

"He said sorry."

Maddie's face brightens and Celia's eyes widen. Great, I've got two of them to answer to now.

"Don't overthink it," I say. "Either of you." I climb onto a white barstool, clutching my purse in my lap.

I'm watching the bartending action when Maddie freezes mid-pour and almost overfills a shaker. She stares behind me, so I assume it must be Devon again. Instead of turning around, I get Maddie's attention instead. "A little heavy on the tequila, don't you think?"

She pulls the bottle upright as Celia reminds her the entire house will be filled with celebrities on Saturday.

Maddie reassures us both. "I'll have it together by then. I promise."

It thrills me that I have more restraint than her right now, but then a firm hand grazes my shoulder and trails down my arm, and I can't even hide the chill it sends through me. Devon leans in close, and I feel his breath on my ear. "Thank you," he says. His hand continues down my wrist, over my fingers, and to my purse, where he opens it and retrieves the envelope. He straightens up and crosses his arms, hiding the envelope between his forearm and abs. Lucky envelope. "So, this afternoon. You in?"

Me? On? I'm turned on, if that's what he means. Oh wait, the yacht. "Yeah. Sure."

"Good. I'll be back later."

I watch him leave and turn back to see both Maddie and Celia staring at me, an incredulous look plastered on their faces. "What?"

Maddie raises an eyebrow and looks down at my purse. "Want to tell me what that was about?"

"I'd love to." I smile. "But it's a Devon Stone secret."

CHAPTER SIXTEEN

By the time my workday is coming to an end, I'm ready to think up any excuse to not go out with Devon tonight. This morning's euphoric high has worn off, and now I keep picturing myself acting stupid on a boat in front of Devon and his friends.

I could tell him I'm not feeling well. Or I can tell him I have too much to do to get ready for his party. Or...

Maddie and Devon come at me in opposite directions. "Ready to go?" they ask in unison.

"Um..." I look at Maddie who's looking at Devon who's looking at me. "Devon, I—"

"Where're you two heading?" Maddie asks.

"He...uh...invited me on his yacht for the evening." I pull my keys from my purse, clutching them tight. Quick. Think of a getaway.

"Oh. Fun!" she says while I plead with her through my desperate glare to help me think up an excuse to get out of it. "I'll need those." She plucks my keys from my hand, knowing damn well she's going to leave me stranded so I have no other choice. "You guys enjoy yourselves."

"Maybe you can come with us?" I say. I'm sure Devon won't mind one more friend. "There will be a group of us, and—"

"Next time. I have to work tonight." She gives me a wicked smile and disappears out the front door, leaving me alone with Devon.

He holds his hand out to me. "Let's go."

Whatever attempt I was going to make to convince myself to stay away from him... All that reasoning vanishes as I reach out my own hand, and our fingers interlock.

After a short drive to a secured marina, we're walking up to a dock. A massive boat awaits and my heart quickens. We could sink. I could fall overboard and drown. I could get seasick and throw up in front of Number Three. I think that covers the worst that can happen.

"It's about time, Stone," says a guy with shaggy blond hair and an eyebrow ring. A girl in the tiniest bikini possible is dangling from one of his arms. They match our pace as we walk by and head toward the water.

"Shut it, Mac," Devon says. "I was waiting for my girl to get off work."

His girl? Since when? Oh well, I'm not correcting him.

Devon steps onto the back of the boat and turns to face me. I hesitate. Running away right this moment would make me an even bigger ass, so there's definitely no way out of it.

"What are you waiting for?" he says, holding his hand out for me to grab. Our fingers intertwine as his hand encases my own, and the next thing I know, I'm standing on the deck of the colossal structure Devon so casually calls *the boat*. It towers over me and every inch is pristine. Solid, dark wood, polished silver, and Stone Label logos inlayed into nearly everything.

And the most beautiful man I've ever laid eyes on is staring at me with the same level of wonder and interest.

"You know how to drive this thing?" I ask Devon.

He laughs and tilts his head forward to motion behind me. "We've got a private crew for that."

I turn around to see two men in sunglasses briskly approaching the yacht. "You've got drivers for everything..."

"I think they prefer to go by Captain and First Mate, but...yeah, it's nice to let others take the wheel so I can...enjoy the scenery."

His eyes are locked on the sheer, black halter dress I'm wearing. His gaze travels up to the straps and across my collarbone. This evening heat is feeling extra hot.

"Come on. You haven't seen anything yet."

And my god, he's right. We go into a room he refers to as the 'lower lobby'. It's bigger than my entire apartment. It's more like a luxury hotel than a boat. I could curl up on one of the couches—they look so plush—and just sleep here until tomorrow. But Devon keeps ahold of my hand and leads me up a set of stairs. I watch him from behind, feeling dazed that this is even happening. I catch a glimpse of another lobby—this one twice the size of my home. He keeps going up to a third level, and the space up here is breathtaking. Couches and a bar and windows lining every wall. I can see the setting sun through the panoramic glass surrounding us.

"How many people can hide in this thing?"

He smiles and answers. "I'm not sure. You'd probably never find them all."

I laugh as Devon's friends take their places around the bar and start setting out glasses and bottles and random other ingredients to start mixing drinks. It's like they own the place, and as overwhelming as this thing is...I can't help but feel myself relax as we pull further away from land. It's like I'm traveling to a new world, living somebody else's life—and that somebody is damn fortunate.

Devon hands me a drink, and I take a sip. Fruity and a little too strong. But I'm on a luxury vacation. I'm going to enjoy every moment.

His own drink in hand, Devon finishes it in seconds and goes for a refill. I sit on one of the window seats staring out at the horizon. It's phenomenal—the sky a canvas of oranges and pinks leading us toward the ends of the Earth.

"You know, the view's even more spectacular outside." Devon sits behind me, not leaving much space at all between us. He speaks quietly into my ear, sending a tingle down my spine. "Want me to show you?"

"I'm okay here. You don't have to."

He places his lips on the back of my shoulder, and his hot breath caresses my skin. "I want to."

I want to too. But my mind is far from the sunset when I look back at him. "Okay."

I take a gulp from my drink, and set the glass on the bar, letting Devon lead the way again. Another flight of stairs, and we're greeted by the open air. "You do understand how ridiculous this boat is, right? Like the friggin' Titanic." *Oh, Olivia. Stupid comment. This is why you shouldn't speak.*

Devon doesn't miss a beat and seems to find me endearing instead of awkward. "Only much smaller and *above* sea level. Come see this."

We're on the sun deck, and he pulls me toward the front of the boat—the *bow*, he explains. I'm learning so much, maybe I can have my own yacht someday...See, I can make jokes.

The front of the deck is tiled with thick cushions. Who needs lounge chairs when you can drop to the ground and be immediately comfortable? A dozen people could sleep on this...easily. Pillows line the edge as though to keep everyone contained. Come to think of it, very kinky things could happen here...and probably have.

I look straight out toward the setting sun and step closer to it like I could touch it. My shins hit the edge of the cushions. I sit down, still staring. All the luxury inside couldn't possibly compare to the natural beauty out here. "Devon. Wow, this is just..." There are no words.

He sits behind me again—his body almost flat against mine. I feel his mouth on my skin, and I can't help but close my eyes. I lean forward as his soft kisses trail along my back and up my neck. My entire body feels electric—alive.

Devon gently nudges my arm to get me to turn around. I scoot back to one of the propped up pillows. Yes, it's all as comfortable as I assumed. I could live here forever. Staring up at Devon, I want him closer. Maybe it's the atmosphere. Maybe it's the liquid courage I was just drinking. But for the first time, I'm not afraid to act on my feelings.

So I do.

CHAPTER SEVENTEEN

I clench the fabric of his shirt in both my fists and pull him down to me. Without hesitation, his lips meet mine. Not soft and slow this time, but quick and with force—like two young lovers about to be caught. He tastes like liquor, and my own light-headedness makes me briefly wonder if this is the right time. I made such a big deal about how we hardly know each other and accused him of wanting only one thing. Yet here I am. A hypocrite. But I'm sick of the push and pull between us. The strange interactions. The stupid arguing. The obvious spark igniting every time we're near each other. Devon kisses my neck, and I stifle a moan. I want more where this came from. Who cares what we think tomorrow? I just want tonight.

I let my hands travel the terrain of his bare chest—my fingers making their own paths along the crevices and smooth plateaus of his toned body. I can feel his pounding heart against the palm of my hand. Oh Devon? Mr. Calm and Cool. You're giving your excitement away. And not just through his quickening pulse. I can feel him growing harder against the inside of my thigh, and I move below him to encourage whatever he wants to do next.

Devon's hand moves down the side of my breast. Down the side of my stomach. Down to my hip, where his powerful fingers grip my flesh as though I'd float away if he let go. I'm locked in place as he presses against me harder. His lips and tongue send electrical shocks wherever they touch—my fingertips. My temple. Behind my ear. My throat. I lick at his lingering taste on my lips as he moves lower. He kisses the skin exposed at the top of my dress. He kisses at the hint of cleavage just above the fabric. He kisses my breast as he hovers over my body, still making his way down.

I'm more alive right now than I've been in years, and it's been a long time since I've been with a guy—not to mention a lifetime since I've been with a guy like Devon.

Just for one night. I'm letting go.

Oh, and I do. Devon kneels in front of me and kisses my bare knee with the lightest touch, as though it's breakable. I use my other leg to hook him from behind and force him closer.

He reaches up with both hands, finding a place for them on either side of my hips. In his firm grasp, I squirm, wanting to beg him for more.

He moves one hand away and a single finger teases the skin at the hem of my skirt. I'd like to rip the whole dress off to make it easier on him, but let's not hurry things. I bend my free leg to run it along his torso. His skin is becoming slick with sweat. I press my foot in between his thighs, rubbing the length of his hardness. I want him in me.

He pushes the fabric of my skirt up, and his fingers meet the silky edge of my thong. I'm exposed to the entire world, and it's exhilarating. I try to focus on steadying my breathing, but each inhale catches as fire sneaks its way through the depths of me.

Without hesitation, he moves up, his mouth just over the thin fabric of my panties. His hot breath cuts straight through to my skin, and my muscles involuntarily stiffen. I'm no longer in control as my hips move forward pleading for him to touch me. To taste me.

He looks me straight in the eyes—his pupils black stone—as he leans down and kisses the silk covering my clit. A moan escapes me, and he grins as he uses his tongue to massage me in slow circles.

I throw my arm over my mouth knowing if he keeps at it, things could get...loud.

His hand runs along the outside of my panties, and I feel myself growing wetter with each stroke. He slips his thumb through one side, and pulls the fabric away. Just as the night breeze hits my bare skin, I hear something.

No.

Footsteps come stomping up from the lower deck, and I jump up to straighten my dress.

No. No. No. No.

Dammit! We were so close to...to something.

But Devon isn't discouraged. He continues to tease me through my dress.

"Hey, someone's coming up here."

"It's okay."

I gulp. "Devon. People are coming. You have to stop."

He obeys, smoothing out my skirt and returning to my side.

"Sorry," I say, as though I told his friends to interrupt.

Devon meets my gaze, his eyes wide and intense. The sun's been replaced by a pitch-black sky sprinkled with stars. Even in the dark, I can see him clearly. He sits up straight and kisses me, softer this time, and the gesture ensures me I have nothing to be sorry about. I wish his friends would leave—go back inside, jump overboard, whatever. But they're settling in their own spots on the lounges that line the rest of the deck. They're too close which means our moment is officially over.

I'm disappointed as Devon takes my hand, tracing his fingers along my own while I try to join our intruders' conversation.

"So Olivia. Our man, Devon, might have convinced you he's a hotshot, but—"

"Don't be an ass, Mac," Devon butts in.

Devon turns to me to see if I want a drink. *I'm good, thanks.* He gets up to help himself at the bar up here. This yacht has everything.

"So what sort of secrets is he hiding from me?" I ask, knowing his friends are probably drunk enough to divulge. The aching in me is tapering off as I find myself returning back to the real world, but I watch Devon at the bar and am tempted to thank the stars above that I agreed to come out here with him. This could be the new normal. I can do this. We could be together.

Devon's friend Mac speaks up again. "You should ask him about the Audi story."

"The what?"

"The Audi story. It's his best one. Never mind, watch this."

Devon rejoins the group, sitting next to me while his friend brings up this supposedly epic story of Devon's past.

"Just tell her about it." Mac—who's proving to be sort of a jerk—turns to me. "And if he tries to make you think he wasn't arrested too, he's full of shit."

I nod. Arrested? Is this what I've been avoiding in the tabloid articles?

"It's nothing," Devon says. "Me, Mac, and Lucas..." He points to his other friend who's been mostly silent all evening. "...We borrowed a car, and it had to be returned."

"Have you gone soft, Dev?" Lucas has a mischievous grin that could compete with Devon's. He's attractive, and his dark eyes and the tattoos on his arms and chest make him look intense. "So one night, we go by Austin's—he's the guy who used to hook us up with good shit, if you know what I mean." I don't. "So Devon always prepaid Austin to keep the supply steady. Plus, the guy didn't talk to the paps, so he was secure. But on this night, Austin doesn't pull through. He's got nothing. So a coked up Devon here decides his money's not to be wasted, and steals his car as retribution. We're following behind the stolen car and stop for some cigarettes a few miles down the road. Devon ends up getting caught with it right in the damn parking lot. Only while Mac and I were inside, he and Kennedy decide to get busy like a couple of fucking rabbits, so he's caught bare ass naked in the backseat."

Lucas is laughing like this is the funniest story ever. My stomach is twisting in a knot. I can't even bring myself to look at Devon who's not even bothering to stop his so-called friend from telling me all this.

Mac takes over and finishes the tale. "But Lucas and I were dipshits and walked back to the car like it's ours anyway. We don't bother to acknowledge the police cruiser parked behind it, and we get snagged up just as quick. Fortunately, your boyfriend has connections, so it ended well."

I nod my head slowly, not looking at Devon. Stolen car. Public sex with his ex. Getting arrested. Cocaine. Ended well?

I don't know what part of all this I like least.

"I think I'll get that drink now."

CHAPTER EIGHTEEN

I stand up before Devon can offer to get it for me. I'm not sure what to think right now. Instead of stopping at the bar out here, I find the stairs and head back inside to the lobby. I just need to be alone for a minute.

God, I'm such an idiot. I knew I should've stayed away, and I was dumb to think I could be with him. I throw some mixture of juice and vodka into a glass. I'm tempted to smash the bottle of liquor against the wall. Or maybe against Devon's head. I knew he was hiding something. Why would I get on a boat with a guy I don't know? Everything about him has screamed that he's trouble, and I followed him around like it could just be ignored.

This room is quiet—peaceful—and I make myself comfortable on one of the plush couches. At some point, the Captain must have turned the boat around because I can see the coastline growing nearer.

After several minutes, I wonder if it's possible Devon could've forgotten about me. I kind of wish that were the case.

"You okay?" he says when he does come looking for me.

Devon comes down the stairs and sits down next to me. He reaches over and brushes a loose strand of hair behind my ear. I flinch, pulling away from him.

"I'm fine."

"Good." He leans over and kisses me, but I push him away.

"Dammit, Devon. Obviously I'm *not* fine." My heart pounds as I try to control how angry I'm feeling. "What the hell was all that?"

"What? The guys? They exaggerate." He runs his hand up my thigh and under my skirt. He reeks of whiskey, and I can't help but wonder if he'll even remember all this tomorrow.

"So make me feel better. Tell me which parts of all that weren't true?"

Devon rolls his eyes and gets up. "Olivia," he says, drawing out each syllable. "You've got to relax."

"What part of that story wasn't true, Devon?"

He sighs and leans against the arm of a couch. His gaze shifts up as he goes back through each detail.

"Tell me," I say again. This time I'm almost pleading. He can't be that person. An addict. A criminal.

"It doesn't matter. It was so long ago."

It was all true. No matter how much I don't want to believe it.

"I can't do this."

"Do what? We were having fun."

"I'm your employee. You're practically my boss. And besides that, I can't be involved with someone who spends his time breaking the law and doesn't seem bothered by it."

"My past, Olivia." Devon stands up and walks to the bar. Great, keep drinking. More points against you. I shake my head just as he turns around and sits on a bar stool instead of going to the other side to play barkeep. "You're telling me you've never fucked up before?"

There's anger in his voice. Just like that first day we met when he was mad at his father. I stare at him with no other response.

"Sorry. Listen, Mac? Lucas? They're assholes."

"They're your friends."

"Sure, but they're assholes I've known all my life. Guys who I've been hanging out with long before people gave a damn about who I was. People like that—who have known you longer than your money and fame—they're hard to come by. I'm sorry for the crap they say. They've never had a filter before. I mean, Kennedy never cared, so..."

"Great. Well, I'm not Kennedy. Maybe you should get back with her."

Devon doesn't bother to keep his voice quiet. "Maybe you're right. You can't do this. And by *this*, I mean act like a grown woman and lighten up."

"Lighten up? Devon, you've got me on some roller coaster, and last I checked, I couldn't handle being spun around without crumbling into a mess. If you actually knew me, you'd know that."

"So everything is perfect in your world?" He yells at me as he crosses his arms in front of him. "You're happy with where you are and who you are? It's all sunshine for you? I'm so glad you've got it all figured out. That makes one of us."

Now I'm livid. He doesn't know the first thing about what my life's been like for me—what I go through on a daily basis. "That's not fair. It's not that easy for me. And whatever you're wanting from me—expecting from me, I can't be that person." I won't be. And who's he to think he's such a victim here? "And what about you? Huh? Am I supposed to just accept it all? Stealing cars? Drugs? Luring in new girls and claiming them as your own?"

He slowly shakes his head. "Wow. Yeah. That's me. Because there's no way I could be genuinely interested in you. No, you're just something I felt like conquering. Please, keep making these assumptions. The double standard here is fucking poetic."

"You haven't giving me much else to work with this week."

"Apparently not." He gets up and heads back toward the stairs to leave. "And I'm not starting now."

CHAPTER NINETEEN

"So you dumped him?"

It's Friday afternoon, and Maddie and I are walking down Rodeo Drive eyeing stores I've always avoided in the past. "We were never dating, so no...I didn't exactly *dump* him. But I'm pretty sure things are done for good."

Maddie pulls me into a tiny boutique called LuxRy. If it weren't for the credit card Celia gave me, one $700 price tag in here would have had me turning and running. Still, I can't help but be shocked by how expensive everything is.

"You've got to look the part, Liv. Embrace it. Be grateful you get to dress cute. I'm stuck in a uniform that makes me feel like a penguin."

She sifts through the assortment of gowns with the focus and haste of a professional. "An open door to a guy that spectacular, and you slam it shut." She shakes her head and pulls a green dress off a rack near the back of the store.

"I'd only intended to, I don't know, prop the door open with a shoe—put things on hold to make sense of it all."

She puts the green one back and grabs a second dress—a vivid, dark purple one and holds the gown high to show me. The silky fabric falls like a waterfall down her arm. "Ooh!" She squeals and thrusts the dress toward me. "It's even on sale. Must be a sign. Go try it on."

I check the tag. Goody, a bargain at $350. Rolling my eyes at Maddie, I take the dress into a fitting room while she returns to the racks to drool over the gowns she won't be buying. Trying this thing on is terrifying. It feels too delicate, like I'm going to rip it apart as I squeeze into it. But it's stronger than it looks, and when I see the result in the mirrors...well, Maddie picked a great dress. Maybe too great. The last thing I want to do is stand out at the party. I'm just there to work, and when it's over, I never have to go back to that house.

I take a breath and prepare for Maddie's overreaction. She's already out there waiting for me, wearing a little black dress that makes her golden hair angelic.

I cross my arms in front of me. "What are you doing?"

"What? I can dream." She reaches over to me, grabbing my hands and stretching my arms out wide. "But you. You look smokin'."

"You think so? I feel like...like I'm not wearing anything." The fabric is cool and thin. Blindfolded, I could almost believe I'm naked. This'll make for an interesting night surrounded by Hollywood's finest.

We change back into our commoner's clothing and check out. I hand my dress to the woman at the register, but instead of taking it, she's just frozen and staring.

Yeah, I know. I don't look like someone who can afford this thing, and the truth is I can't. But hello? I'm right here. Ready to pay.

"I'd like to buy this." I push the dress even closer to her.

She blinks and steps back, taking the dress like she's just stepped out of a trance. Maddie and I finish paying and leave the store.

"That was weird. Are we not a high enough status to be shopping in there? Did you see the way she stared at us?"

"She wasn't eyeing you like you were some second class citizen. She recognized you." She stops and pulls her phone out. "You saw today's headline, right?"

"I'm avoiding that stuff."

Maddie hands me the phone, and I'm staring at a photo of myself. In it, Devon's holding my hand and leading me onto the yacht. A bright yellow headline screams: "If the Boat's A'Rockin' Don't Come A'Knockin'—Devon Stone Sets Sail with His Newest Love Interest!"

I thrust the phone back at Maddie. "Are they kidding me? As if I didn't already feel awful about this whole thing, they make it seem like something it definitely is not?"

She laughs and we start walking again. "It's what they do. They've outed you as Devon's girlfriend. It's no secret now."

Click.

That familiar sound of the camera shutter comes from behind us, and I whip my head around to see a man following with a fat, gaudy lens concealing most of his face.

"Dammit. How did I get myself into this?" I shield myself and walk faster.

"By getting involved with Devon Freakin' Stone, of all people. You need to accept it."

Click, click.

"No. After last night, I'm not accepting anything."

She puts an arm around my shoulders. "You don't really think things are over, do you? You even said yourself that you didn't break up."

"Because we were never dating. There was nothing to break up. He's just...not what I'd thought he'd be."

"Oh sweetie, this guy's always been trouble. He's even got sexy mugshots and—"

Click.

I glare at the paparazzi vulture. *Click.* "I don't want to talk about it. After the party, I don't have to see him again, so we'll just forget about it all."

She nods and changes the subject. Maddie's good at knowing when I'm serious about something. And don't think I haven't considered what to do about Devon. He haunted me the entire night after we went our separate ways. I had been so pissed, yet I couldn't stop thinking about him. The way he kissed me. The way he made me feel like I fit right into his world. The way his mouth felt on my thighs. The dreams that came from that alone were enough to drive me mad.

But it was all a joke. With Bryce...we broke up because I couldn't handle his constant trips to Vegas. He loved gambling. Not that he was addicted or anything, but I felt like it was only a matter of time. I'd calculated the risks of staying with him—thought of all the possible ways it could end terribly—and I knew I'd have to leave him.

The threat I felt back then was purely hypothetical. Devon...it's all too real. He'd already passed the point of being a deal breaker for me. Now he was just a gorgeous man waving around tons of red flags featuring bold, black print: *Stay away!*

"Let's eat here." Maddie grabs my hand and pulls me into a deli with no warning. I almost tumble to the ground. "Sorry, I noticed that camera guy was looking down for a second. This was our quick escape."

"Thanks. I appreciate that. Can you imagine the people who have to deal with that every day of their lives?"

"Yeah," Maddie says, a dreamy sound in her voice. "It could be fun."

Of course she'd find the fun in that.

We order food and find a quiet table in a corner, and Maddie picks up where she left off as though the conversation hadn't ended. "You're telling me you wouldn't love the attention from people who think you're amazing?"

"But I'm not amazing." I laugh. "If they only knew."

"Oh, but you are. You're Devon Stone's girlfriend."

I kick her under the table. "I am not—"

"You *are* her."

A random girl and her friend appear at our table. She pulls out a chair and sits down as if to join us. I don't even know what to say. Is she serious?

She continues, "I thought it was you. But it wasn't until she just said it that I realized, like, wow, you *are* her. So what's he really like? God, he's so hot. You have no idea how lucky you are."

"I'm...um..." Just then our food shows up. I have no way out of this.

Maddie stops the server before he places anything down. "Actually, we need that to go. Sorry."

Thank you. I owe you. I try to push all my grateful thoughts into her mind. I'm sure she gets it anyway. I still don't know what to tell these gawking girls, and then—

Click.

The damn photographer's found us too.

Crawling under the table probably wouldn't save me, so I'm left with either running away or blocking myself from his view.

At least I've got Maddie. But she can't possibly understand why I'm beginning to tremble and can't seem to catch my breath. No, this is my nightmare, and mine alone.

One of the girls squeals and beams at her friend standing behind her. "Yes! We'll be in the picture, Zoe. Oh my god. We'll be in a magazine." Her friend seems just as excited. They take turns checking each other's makeup and taking care of stray strands of hair while I duck down in my seat, angling away from the noise of the camera shutter.

Click. Now when these dimwits speak, they do it with huge, exaggerated smiles. "Ok, now what we really want to know. Like, we've seen what he looks like without a shirt. There was even that picture of him in his underwear. But, like..." She lowers her voice but is still grinning like a lunatic. "How *altered* were those photos, if you know what I mean?"

"You know what?" Maddie speaks up for me again. I owe her my life. Seriously, best friend ever. "Her and Devon's private life is none of your business. So keep using your imagination rather than confronting his girlfriend about personal information."

No Maddie. You're supposed to clarify I'm not with him! Set things straight before things grow out of control.

Maddie stands up as the server brings our food in to-go bags. She leans over the sitting girl in an attempt to be more intimidating. "So scurry along now. You two should be happy enough you met her." I could hug Maddie for being so badass right now, never mind her inaccurate information.

The quieter girl, Zoe, huffs and rolls her eyes. "Whatever. It's not like they'll last."

"Yeah," the other one says. "Besides, he might see the pictures that guy's taking, see me, and realize he can do much better."

Maddie steps even closer to the girl, unafraid of getting right in her face. "*Actually,* they're very much in love. They're perfect together. So trust me, there's nothing..." She dramatically scans the girl up and down.

"...*Nothing* you could give him that would come close to how great Olivia is for him."

Dammit, Maddie.

CHAPTER TWENTY

My alarm goes off for the second time. 5:10. We should have left for the party ten minutes ago, so naturally I'm about to have an aneurysm.

"What the hell's taking you so long?" Unsteady in heels, I march to Maddie's room and bang on her door. It swings open, and I find her in front of a mirror adding smoky makeup to her eyes while music blares from her computer. "You're making us late. I'm about to leave without you."

"Relax. I'm stuck in this stupid uniform. I have to find some way to stand out."

She straightens up and turns toward me. She's sporting the same white blouse and black skirt as the other female staff, but she's added a thin, silky red scarf and has her hair curled and pulled to one side.

"Adorable," I say. "Now get in the car before I regret ever getting you the job."

She snatches a small clutch from her bed. "Somebody's a bit touchy tonight."

I ignore her and leave the apartment, impatiently holding the door for her so I don't have to wait for her to lock up.

Once we're on the road, she's checking her red lips in the rearview mirror. "Who do you think we'll see tonight?"

"Hungry and thirsty people." My backup alarm for my backup alarm begins to buzz. "Get that for me, please."

I hear a huff as she reaches over to my bag to find my phone. "Dr. Shannon said—"

"Leave it for Dr. Shannon to say. This has been a weird week, okay?"

"Yes. It's been a strange and unpredictable few days for you, and yet look, you're still alive. Still breathing." She silences the alarm and leans back in her seat.

"That doesn't mean it's been easy." I shouldn't have to defend myself. My habits don't affect anybody except myself. Sure, they've affected my jobs and relationships and my tendency to lock myself in my room for days at a time, but it's not hurting anyone else.

"Life isn't always easy, Liv." She tangles her hair around her fingers as she starts lecturing me. "We all have our battles, and we all deal with them in different ways. We don't avoid excitement and life experiences just because of unexpected bumps in the road."

"Right. And what's your battle exactly?" Maddie gleefully left home at seventeen, eager to live on her own. She's beautiful and has a carefree dating life. Her job allows her to have fun and make enough money. I rarely see her in a bad mood, so I can hardly believe she's dealing with too many demons.

But she lets out a choke of a laugh. "Do you seriously think I grew up daydreaming about mixing cocktails for drunk people? Getting hit on by pushy men? Damn Olivia, we live in the same apartment, so you know I'm not exactly living in luxury. I moved a thousand miles away from my family to make it big like every other failed actress in this place. I've spent plenty of time second-guessing my choices and putting myself down for thinking I could amount to anything. I should have been like you. I should've gone to college, stayed closer to home, been more grateful for the life I had. But now it's too late to go back because then they'd all know my high hopes were a disaster. So I'm Happy Maddie. Things are just peachy. No battles here."

We drive in silence for the next few minutes. Now I feel bad. How many times this week have I made assumptions that have come

back to bite me in the ass? First with Devon—
more than once. Now with my own best
friend. I'm on a roll.

"I'm sorry," I finally say. "I've always ad-
mired you and how easy you make it all seem.
It never even occurred to me that..."

"It's okay," she says. "It's why I want more
for you. I know you can break your old habits.
If you let go of your obsessions and try new
things, maybe you'll feel more comfortable
with yourself. And more fulfilled with your
life."

It sounds nice, but...

Maddie keeps going, "You have to start
small though. Stop with the incessant alarms
that dictate what you do and when. Then stop
overanalyzing every detail. No stringent routine or cell phone reminder can tell you who
to be. Take control. It's your life to live. Try
being impulsive. Some spontaneity can go a
long way."

She says it like I avoid all those things, but
I don't. I mean, look at this week with Devon.

Everything I've done with him has been over-the-top and mostly unplanned. *And look where it got you.* I basically accused him of being a criminal and a man-whore. Not that he didn't supply plenty of evidence to back those claims, but even when I tried to let go the other night on the yacht, it backfired. Now I don't know where we stand.

"The internet seems to think I'm the girl-friend of one of the richest celebrities in the country. How's that for starting small?"

"It doesn't matter what they think. What's the truth?"

I shake my head as I near the entrance to the Stone mansion. Both sides of the road are lined with cars and people. Tons of paparazzi with their obnoxious cameras, of course. But there are others. Fans? Some look like every-day people out for a walk, but others are dressed extra nice, like they're hoping for a last second invitation inside. A few people even hold signs that shout bold-lettered salu-tations to the different celebrities they expect to be in attendance. I've seen these same groups of people alongside the red carpet coverage on TV. In person, it's bizarre. But what's even more surreal is how Maddie and I easily approach the gates, get a quick nod from Roger, and effortlessly gain access into one of the most coveted events of the year.

"The truth is..." I'm afraid to admit how much fun I'm having. Being known as Devon's girlfriend—being recognized as such? I want that. I want him. But what comes with that? The hassle, the exposure, the lack of privacy, the world knowing who I am. "I don't know if I can do it."

CHAPTER TWENTY-ONE

We're probably the only people pulling in and parking our own car, and better yet, my little sedan stands out like a pimple on prom night. We pull to the side of the house where few will even notice us, and the second I step out of the car, I twist my left ankle. *That took no time at all.* And just as my poor feet were finally feeling better from the last time I braved heels. I knew it would happen, but there's no way I'd get away with wearing ballet flats in this dress at this party. Walking inside, through a side door leading straight into the kitchen, I try to hide my limp. It's too early for this.

All was quiet outside, but inside, it's bustling with chaos already. Our catering chefs are preparing the first trays of hors d'oeuvres to be ready the moment our guests arrive. Plates and glasses are being polished to perfection as others carry cases of bottles to the party room. Celia is standing in the center of the room supervising everyone's work when she spots us coming in.

"Oh, my girls are here!"

I rush over ready with excuses. "I'm so sorry we're late. We must have underestimated the time we needed, and then we were held up by—"

Celia grips each of my shoulders. "Whoa there. Lighten up. You're at a party!" She points Maddie and I toward the door leading out into the ballroom. "Let's start with drinks."

We head toward the bar to get Maddie set up at her post. The house isn't too crowded yet, but it's early. The deejay is playing a quieter indie song, and the guests that have arrived are in clusters speaking in hushed tones. A few servers with trays offer them food on little white plates.

At the bar, staff mixes drinks, and Maddie excitedly hurries to her side of the high top counter. I hand her my purse to hide underneath along with her own.

I expect Celia to give me some sort of task next, but instead, she says, "A round of shots. Let's go with Fireball to get us started on a good note."

As though there's nothing odd about the request, Maddie pours a couple ounces of amber liquid into glasses, and we each take one.

"Are you sure this is a good idea? I mean, we're working, and..." I trail off as both women drain theirs in unison and stare at me waiting.

"If you'd rather deal with tonight completely sober, that's your call," Celia says. "You're about to deal with half of Hollywood, your boyfriend, and Keenly, who's in quite the mood. You should have seen him throwing a tantrum earlier about the centerpieces—something about roses and incompetence."

The orchids. I can't help but smile about that. *Thanks Devon.*

"Say no more." I empty my own glass, wincing from the brief burning of cinnamon. "I've never been a more awful employee."

Celia laughs, "Consider it personality reinforcement. You've got to have a great face at these parties to blend in with the guests. Liquor makes that easier, so the way I see it, we all owe it to our jobs."

"And what exactly is my job here tonight?"

She glances around the room like she's undercover and looking for anything suspicious. "We will be making sure everything is running smoothly. So mingle. Wander through the crowds. Make sure the food is fresh, the guests are happy, and the staff is smiling. That's all."

"That's all..." I look around. There are so many beautiful people here. Women wear gowns that must be custom-made to fit only their bodies, and they sparkle from an array of jewels. They're flawless—the diamonds *and* the women. The men are sporting the nicest tuxes I've ever seen. This isn't some high school dance. Everyone is a cookie cutter copy of a magazine cover. This really is the easiest paycheck I've ever made. I could see myself making a career out of this assistant to the assistant thing.

After my first round through the party, I drop into one of the stools across from Maddie to rest my throbbing feet. My hurt ankle shoots pain up through my leg and reminds me of sitting outside with Devon by the pool and him plunking my feet into the cold water. I haven't seen him here tonight. Did he skip the party? Did he do it because of me?

"Need another shot?" Maddie asks me while simultaneously pouring Scotch on the rocks, handing it to a server, and getting an order from a guest who looks familiar. I can't pinpoint him though. After serving him his requested Bourbon cocktail, she pours a clear liquid into a glass and sticks it in front of me without waiting for my answer.

I shake my head. I really shouldn't, but the first shot is making me feel more relaxed. Maybe a second would make it easier to ignore my ankle. I drink it quickly knowing I'll probably regret it. "You know, I can't name most the people here. You'd think my mind wouldn't be drawing blanks."

"It's your nerves. Let me help. She tilts her head toward the guy she just served. Werewolf Chronicles. Cole Hudson."

"Holy shit, it is!" I say that a little too loudly and clasp a hand over my mouth. Cole-effing-Hudson is two stools down talking to some other guy. I've only ever seen him on his show, and I don't watch it that often. In person, he's got more tattoos than I remember, and he's much taller.

"Over by the side wall," Maddie says.

I follow her gaze. "Bia," I answer. And holy hell, it is. The internationally famous pop singer is accepting a plate of food from one of the servers while talking to a woman I don't recognize. "Who's that with her?"

"Hayley Wade. Remember that old band Seventh Inferno? Her dad was that Razor guy."

"Didn't he just die?" Hayley doesn't look like she's mourning. Then again, maybe she relies on the same *personality reinforcements* as the Platinum Planning staff.

"He did. But I don't think they were that close. Besides, she's with Kaidan."

"Devon's brother?" I turn back to Maddie and can almost predict exactly what she's about to say.

"Yep. So screw you both. My chances with a Stone brother are ruined."

I laugh at her predictability while she pretends to pout.

"Maybe they have another sibling we don't know about hiding under the staircase or something."

"One can only hope. Speaking of, don't turn around, but your man is here." She tilts her head forward indicating he's somewhere behind me.

I turn anyway and find myself frozen. He's stayed true to his 'don't-give-a-damn' style, wearing a sleek, dark gray suit jacket over a vintage t-shirt and designer jeans. Even being the most underdressed person here, he still seems to fit right in. Surrounded by a cluster of guests, they're all focused on him, entranced by whatever he's saying.

I find myself smiling. I can't help it. Someone as relaxed and natural as he is, he has a presence that can make anyone feel secure and important.

As if he can hear my thoughts, he looks up from the group and immediately meets my eyes. I'm equally relieved and distressed that he showed up. At some point, I'll have to confront him. But now's not that time. I break our eye contact and turn to Maddie. "That reminds me. I have work to do."

I get up and quickly walk the opposite direction from him. Intending to check on the guests in the party room upstairs, my foot barely hits the bottom step when I hear someone come up from behind me.

"Hello again, lovely."

CHAPTER TWENTY-TWO

I turn to find Calvin Stone swiftly approaching. I'm not exactly relieved as I take note of the glazed look in his droopy eyes and his sloppy grin. *Not like Devon at all.*

"Hi," I say meekly and take a step away to leave. "I don't think we've formally met. I'm Olivia."

He takes my hand and kisses it. "Of course we've met, sweet thing. Were you on your way to meet me upstairs."

I back away. Clearly, I'm not who he thinks I am. "Umm, no. I'm going back to the kitchen to work."

I start to walk away, but he follows closely. Who knew this huge foyer could feel so tiny?

"Not so fast," he slurs. "You look like you need a Calvin hug, don't ya?"

"No, I'm fine. Thank you though." Gross.

He doesn't take no for an answer and steps in front of me. I'm between him—reeking of liquor—and the cool wall behind me. He presses his hand to the wall, his fingers inches from my head. He reminds me of high school boys leaning against their lockers, gazing at their cheerleader girlfriends. It only makes this creepier.

"I'd love to see that pretty mouth smile," he says quietly. I try to hide my revulsion. "It's a shame I'm with my sweet, true love, Serena. You and I could have had a good time together."

I say nothing. I mean, what the hell is he doing? He takes my silence as an invitation to continue.

"Are you one of Greg's people?" Now it makes sense that he's old friends with Keenly—a creeper and an asshole. "Great party here tonight. Good work."

I clear my throat. "Thank you. I'm not sure Devon's as excited for tonight though." Where'd that come from? Devon made his distaste for this event pretty clear, but who am I to throw him under the bus? I said it before I could even think it. Adrenaline? Alcohol? Whichever, now that it was out in the open, I anticipated his reaction.

"That's because my young son would rather see us all fail. He's never possessed the same—shall I say—pureblood determination and boldness of other Stones. He wouldn't know how to take the lead even if he wanted to—"

"Is that right?"

I jump at his voice. Devon walks up from behind his father and roughly pulls his arm from the wall, knocking the old man back a few steps. "What the hell do you think you're doing?"

"This is my home, son. I'll do as I damn well please."

"And I'm sure your *girlfriend* would approve." He walks past his father so he's standing in front of me, his face inches from Calvin's. "Don't ever go near Olivia again. Do you understand me?"

Without waiting for a response, he takes my hand and leads me upstairs. We walk past the busy party room, and I can't ignore all the heads that turn in our direction. Devon brings me halfway down a dark hallway and stops abruptly.

"Are you okay?"

"I'm fine."

I'm not fine. At all. But it hardly has anything to do with Calvin Stone. All my thoughts about this week are rushing back all

at once. Looking at Devon, it's too obvious
there's more to him than being laid back and
charismatic. No, he's trouble. To be with him
would mean letting go of control—forgetting
exactly who I need to be. I've already seen it
happen. Getting distracted. Acting carelessly.
Giving into lust at the first opportunity. I
can't be that person.

"I'm so sorry about him," Devon says.
"When it comes to women, he's scum. He can
run a business like no other—the fucking
king of the music industry. But he's mostly
just a sleaze bag in his private life."

"I don't care about your dad. He's not the
problem."

"Then what is?" He sounds angry, and I
don't know if it's because of his father or if
our previous fight is reigniting.

What *is* the problem? He's right here when
there's a house filled with glamorous, gorgeous women—many of which wouldn't have
to think twice about being with him. God, I
want him. But wanting isn't enough. The

nagging voice inside my brain has been re-peating itself for days.

We'd never work.

I need to be honest with him and tell him whatever was building between us—it's through. "I've been thinking about the other night. And...and maybe I was too quick to as-sume, but your past is all I know about you. And you know even less about me, so believe me when I say...I just don't think we could ev-er..."

"You're not the only one who gets to make that decision."

"Devon, I'm nothing like those people down there. I—"

"Don't you get it? That's why I'm falling for you."

He's what?

"That's crazy," I argue. "You can't—"

"Believe *me* when I say I've done crazier. But I'm falling for a girl I hardly know. A girl I want to know. A girl who's making it harder and harder to get to know." He pushes his hair away from his forehead, and the scent of his shampoo drifts toward me. "You have some pre-conceived idea of who I am. I know my past doesn't help. I don't deny I'm a screw-up, Olivia. The headlines—my family— remind me constantly. So I can't blame you for wanting to run. But I don't have much more energy in me to keep trying to make this work."

And now silence. It's my turn to speak. But I wasn't expecting that. He wants to make things work. But... "Make what work?"

"That's what I want to know too."

I don't have the right response. I can give this a chance and pray my insecurities don't get the best of me. I can let him go and probably never see him again. Neither sounds ideal.

"Devon, I don't know—"

"That's the second thing. *You* need to lighten the hell up."

Is he kidding? He goes from admitting his feelings for me to insulting me? "Right, so I'm the problem? I—"

"You need to let go of these petty issues of yours. You're beautiful. You're smart. You're an adult. You're capable. Stop acting like you don't know any of these things. If I have to repeat it to you, fine. But it would be much easier if you'd just cut yourself a damn break. Maybe then you'd stop hiding from life."

First Maddie. Now Devon. Are they teaming up behind my back?

"Are you even listening, or am I wasting my—"

"Yes. I'm listening." No, he wants me to react on impulse. Like he does. He'd rather I spouted out my every thought rather than considering things, making careful decisions. Maybe he's the one who needed to learn how to give things time and listen more. "Is there a third thing?"

"Yeah, there is." Without giving me a chance to predict what he'd say next, Devon closes the gap between us, his mouth meeting mine with a desperate force. His hands fall to my shoulders, and as soon as they touch my skin, they seem to come to life. His arms wrap around me, and his fingers grip my bare skin, pressing me into him even more. Even his hands act as though this could be it for us. Our tongues dance, and his lips make promises I desperately need him to keep.

I pull away to catch my breath and find myself laughing. "Right. Number Three. That's you." Shit. I say it before remembering my oath to never admit I'd seen "The Lust List".

He gives me a disapproving look. "You do read that smut."

"No. No. Maddie told me. I had no idea before then. Didn't even know who you were. I swear, I—"

His devilish smile lets me know I'm off the hook. He licks his lips and brings his face close to mine again. This time his lips graze my cheek and move to my ear.

My own hands find their way to the back of his neck and up into his hair—his dark strands intertwining with my pale skin. His entire body is warm. Firm. Everywhere.

He wants me.

Every inch of him is trying to prove it, and I want, more than anything, to give in.

But I can't.

I break away from him.

"It won't."

"What won't what?"

"*We.* We won't work. No matter how much we try to force it, it would never last."

"You don't even want to give it a shot?" His eyebrows furrow as he rubs the bridge of his nose with his fingers. "I don't get it, Olivia. For a second, we're on the same page, and then—"

"We're in different universes?" I look down the hall and then back up at him. "This is your world. And I don't fit in. You have everything. No worries. Family. The opportunities to do anything you want."

"You haven't seen my world." He spreads out his arms as though showing something off. "You've seen my dad's. And my family? My dad's a perverted sociopath dating a woman who's younger than I am, and my brother's his shadow. Don't even get me started on him."

"Be lucky yours is alive."

"He—What? What's that mean?"

"Sorry. I didn't mean to bring it up. I had a brother. He died. You should be more grateful." I'm cursing Celia and Maddie for giving me those shots. The dumbest things keep escaping my mouth.

He reaches up to touch my face and keeps his voice quiet. "I want you to let me into your life. I want to know these things about you. I want to be the one to help you cope with whatever's happened to you."

"But all this isn't for me. We're not right together."

He drops his arm and turns away. I can sense he's trying to stay calm, deciding what to say next. He comes back to stand in front of me, his eyes full of sincerity. "I can't do this back and forth thing. Just tell me, one way or the other, and we'll go from there. When I wake up tomorrow, will you be in my life?"

He makes it sounds so simple. Like I can split my life in between being a Hollywood girlfriend and a broke college graduate. Like I can just change everything about me to feel more confident in going forward with this. I don't know how to answer him, so all I can say is, "I can't."

"Fine." He turns and leaves before I can finish my thought.

I can't.

I can't tell you one way or the other.

I can't explain why this is so hard.

I can't decide at this moment whether there's a future for us.

But those two words were enough of an answer. Tears sting my eyes as I try to pull myself together. It's better this way. I don't understand my whirlwind attraction for him.

Like a magnet. Or a deadly trap. Maybe I'm lucky I narrowly missed an uncertain fate.

Unsure where Devon disappeared to, I hurry downstairs to get busy with some other task. I need to work. I need this party to speed up. I need to go home and never have to come back again.

The faster this night comes to an end, the faster I can forget this entire week ever happened.

CHAPTER TWENTY-THREE

It's strange walking back into a jubilant atmosphere—the party in full swing—and not one soul in here knows what all I've just been through. Well, except Calvin, who sits at the head table, his very young, very bleach-blond-haired girlfriend attached to his arm. A new drink is brought to him right as he finishes the old one, and he gives a nod and a wink to his server before returning to his conversation. My stomach flops, and I feel sick.

I end up back at Maddie's bar. She's talking to a cute, blond guy with a lip ring. One look at me, and she turns back to the mystery man and says something to him. He hands her his cell phone, and—as though she's done it a million times before—she adds in her information in seconds and hands it back with a smooth smile. The guy brushes his lips against her cheek, and I think I see her blush. Then he walks away and she comes over to me.

"Did you just send him away?"

"Yeah," she says, shrugging. "He knows how to find me. What's up?"

"I talked to him."

"Who?" she asks, and I give her a *look* that tells her it should be obvious. "Need a third?"

Third. Number Three. Devon.

But she's talking about a drink. "No. I need to be able to walk straight." Particularly since I can't even think straight.

Maddie's in her zone, clearly enjoying herself, when a tall girl walks up, and Maddie's eyes grow wide. As glamorous as everyone is here, this woman still manages to stand out— probably because of the mermaid-like hair cascading down her back. The top is the same icy blue as Devon's eyes, and the ends transition to a gradient of blues and greens. It's striking and bold, and when she turns my way, her porcelain skin and charcoal eye shadow give her away.

"The one and only, Kennedy Rose," Maddie exclaims. "I was at a Tempest Ultra show last year. You were great."

Perfectly-fucking-perfect. Devon's ex is here. Does she know who I am? Considering she's looking past me like I don't exist, I think it's safe to say my identity hasn't been uncovered. She catches me staring at her, smiles, and turns to Maddie.

"Thanks. You ladies don't mind if I hang out here for a bit, do you? This is all a little much for me." She nods her head toward the center of the room with the throngs of people. I can't say I disagree.

"Pick your poison," Maddie says and quickly gets to work making her a vodka-Red Bull.

Kennedy takes a sip and visibly relaxes in her seat. I should give her a chance. Maybe she's nice.

"These Stones. Everything's got to be monumental with them. Their possessions. Their events. Their relationships."

"You dated Devon, didn't you?" Maddie asks, and I shoot her a deadly glare. What the hell is she doing?

"For two years." She nods. "We had something other couples don't." She looks right at me. "It's like, we were always on the same wavelength, you know?"

No, I don't know.

"It takes a hell of a woman to wrangle these guys. There's nothing easy about being a part of the Stone family." She gulps more of her drink. "Quiet, mousey girls would never survive." She stares out toward the party, scanning the room until her eyes stop on one spot. Devon.

I'm not an idiot. I can read through her lines, so it's obvious she does know me. What is she trying to accomplish here? "Sorry to hear things ended for you."

"I'm sure you are." She gives me a once over, glowering. "I'm curious. How did you do it? I give him two years of my life, yet it takes you two days to convince him to waste his time on you?"

"I must be a hell of a woman."

She laughs. "Somehow I doubt that. It's okay. He may like you now, but he loved me. So when he gets bored with you—"

"Like he got bored with you?" Maddie leans across the bar toward Kennedy. "Devon dumped you how long ago? Yet you're here tonight still chasing after him? That's a little...pathetic, don't you think?"

Kennedy stands up and steps back from the bar, but Maddie comes around from the other side and stands next to me.

"Leave my friend alone. She's got way more to offer than you ever did. You're just the old girlfriend. Old news. As worn out as your last single."

Kennedy's gaze turns hard, and she holds her head up higher. "That's too bad. You seemed cool," she says to Maddie. "I was going to put you on my VIP list, but it looks like you're no better than her." She stomps away from us but she's moving toward Devon. I don't think we've made anything better here.

I turn to Maddie. "I thought you liked her and her music."

"Oh, I love her stuff." She returns behind the bar and gets back to work like nothing ever happened. "But I love you more."

I should feel grateful, but I can't deny my own anger. I'm mad at Kennedy for being a bitch. Mad at Devon for making all this happen. Mad at myself for not being able to handle my problems myself. And mad at Maddie for knowing that about me.

"What is it?" She's looking at me, waiting for my reaction to everything that just happened.

"You shouldn't have done that."

"What? She was trying to tear you down. I wasn't going to stand here and watch it."

"I have to take care of myself. Instead, everyone's always saving me..." I scan the room and find Devon. He's near the stage with his brother, a few others, and Kennedy. Ugh. "What's so wrong with me that I can't handle my own life?"

"Nothing's wrong with you. You just...sometimes need some support. And those of us who care about you will continue to be there—no matter what—until you find your own strength."

The clinking of crystal interrupts us as the three Stone men take to the stage.

"Good evening, friends." Calvin has a microphone in one hand and his girlfriend in the other. She looks like she's barely legal, and I'm pretty sure she's only with him because he signed her to Stone Records and made her a worldwide hit.

As Calvin speaks, Serena and her plastered smile gaze up at him lovingly. Awkward doesn't begin to describe it. But this is the Hollywood big leagues. Who am I to judge?

He's talking about the history of the label and how it's time to pass down the torch to the next Stone to take the throne. I notice Devon and his brother standing off to the side. Kaidan is relaxed, his hands folded in front of him. Devon, on the other hand, has put distance between he and his brother and is barely paying attention to what his father says. Instead, he stares into a half empty glass of something, tilting it slowly as though watching the ice move is more interesting to him.

Calvin Stone continues to talk about the "love of his life", Serena Lynn, and how his retirement means the start of their happily ever after. I couldn't make this up if I tried. It's almost gag-worthy, but there's some real puppy love-like bliss emanating from their little stage.

He keeps talking for some time, but I'm distracted by Devon. He seems nervous, focused on his hands as he fumbles with his drink. Party guests are constantly blocking my view, but each time I catch a glimpse of him, he seems more and more distraught. I haven't seen this in him before. So far, he's either been carefree or pissed off, but he's remained undeniably sure of himself. I want to comfort him. I want to be closer. To know what's wrong. To help him. But it's just as well. What would I be able to do? Especially with Kennedy waiting off to the side.

Applause erupts all around as Calvin announces Kaidan Stone as the next President of Stone Records and moves to the side to let his son take the stage. Kaidan is definitely Devon's brother. They have the same dark hair and mischievous eyes. The same brooding pout. The *favorite* son. He stands tall and proud, the image of a businessman—an incredibly attractive businessman. He takes the microphone from his father and delivers a speech that honors his dad's legacy and hard work while showing gratitude for being chosen to take his place—as though it were a surprise. Devon had known all along, so I'm sure Kaidan had as well. Nonetheless, he puts on a great face, and everyone is excited that he's inheriting an empire of which I can hardly imagine.

"So once again, thank you," he says. "It's an honor I'll never take for granted. And now I know my wonderful brother, Devon, who has always had my back—my greatest supporter, would like to say a few words."

My heart jumps, and my attention is focused on that stage. Devon steps up, and I feel nervous *for* him.

"Yeah. I don't have much to say," he says, taking a sip of his drink before he continues. "We all knew it was coming, so I offer my congratulations to my brother. You earned it." He pats him on the shoulder. "All those years of being a loyal lapdog to our father. They've finally paid off in your favor. I admire you for never following your own dreams or having your own opinions—instead doing whatever our old man wanted you to. That's over two decades of kissing ass, in case anyone was counting. I'm sure having everything handed to you on a platter will be everything you hoped it would be and more. And congratulations to my father and the lovely Serena." He turns away from his audience and toward his family. "I'm sure I'll be calling you mom someday." He turns back to his audience, most people drunk enough they're laughing, unfazed by the resentment dripping from Devon's every word. But Serena looks stunned and confused. Calvin is clenching his jaw and glaring at his son. And Kaidan shakes his head and sighs. Devon finishes the last of his drink and places the mic back on its stand. "There you have it. The perfect family right there. Cheers."

His steps waver as he walks off the stage and through the crowd, toward the bar. Toward me.

FIRST TASTE

CHAPTER TWENTY-FOUR

He stops in front of me and reaches out, gripping my arm with his hand. I'm not sure if it's because he's so drunk he needs support to stay upright or if this is one more plea for me to reciprocate his affection. My skin warms where his fingers touch, and he stares at me like his own survival depends on my eye contact. "Last chance, Olivia."

He's right here. *Do something.*

Every part of me wants to give in. Let the universe take control. We could be Devon and Olivia. We could top the tabloids. Evade the paparazzi. Make everyday an adventure.

But I lower my gaze. I hesitate. And he lets go.

He rushes off and slams through the kitchen door, most likely escaping out the side of the house. A blur of movement catches my attention as Kennedy goes after him. She looks at me, giving me a sly smile, right before she disappears too.

I swing toward Maddie who shrugs her shoulders. "It's your move," she says.

"We couldn't be more different. It could never work."

"No. That's exactly why it *might* work."

She can't possibly be right.

As if she has to dumb it down for me, I hear her say, "You want him. Go get him."

I stop myself from thinking and let my legs do the work instead. I make my way into the kitchen, heading toward the side door. Devon's out there somewhere. But so's Kennedy.

"Miss Margot. Are you just now joining us?"

Mr. Keenly.

The rodent of a man walks over to me shaking his head in disapproval. "If I had to guess, I'd say you've been useless to Celia all this time as well."

Not now, you asshole. I look out the windows trying to see anything outside, but it's too dark.

"Am I keeping you from something more important?" Keenly asks in a condescending tone.

As a matter of fact, yes. You are. I feel trapped. I'm working. But I can't let Devon go, and I definitely can't let Kennedy go with him.

Keenly starts lecturing me about the values of hard work. About how important all these people are, and how I should have never been allowed to work among them. But my thoughts are even louder than his condescending voice. I'm in control. I don't need everyone else to tell me what to do or when to do it. I need to live my life. Be spontaneous. Be impulsive. Don't let people stomp all over me.

This night has been bullshit. Hell, this entire week.

Devon.

His awful friends.

Kennedy.

The paparazzi.

Those girls at the cafe.

And Greg Keenly—my asshole boss.

Only I can decide how the rest of this night goes.

"You know what? I don't have to listen to this."

Keenly's hand flies to his chest like I've shot him. "Excuse me. Is that any way to speak to your superior?"

"You'll never be my superior." I move toward the door. I have to get out of here.

"I will not tolerate that sort of insubordination."

I open the door.

"Miss Margot. You leave this room, and you are fired."

"Fuck off, Keenly. I quit."

I rush out of the house, exhilarated and wild. What the hell did I just do? I feel light, like a Keenly-sized weight has been lifted. Now where's Devon?

He could've left already. I wouldn't blame him. But rounding the corner of the house, walking toward the front, I see him pacing near the fountain.

Kennedy's halfway to him, sauntering toward him as though she can seduce him with her strut.

I don't think so, bitch.

"Devon," I call, quickening my pace, trying to ignore the shooting pain in my feet. Damn these heels. I stop and kick off both shoes, stooping down to scoop them up with one hand.

Devon quits pacing and looks in my direction. Or is he looking at Kennedy? He starts walking, and Kennedy and I both freeze waiting to see what he's doing—who he chooses.

My heart almost stops as he nears Kennedy. But then he walks past, and I don't even hide my happiness. I walk the last few steps to meet him and throw my arms around him.

"I was afraid you'd left before I could—"

He kisses me, his mouth crashing into me, cutting off my words. I pull him into me wanting to disappear into his arms forever. When he breaks away, I look behind him and watch as Kennedy stomps back through the front door, slamming it behind her.

"Do you need to go back in and work?"

I shake my head. "I just quit my job."

Devon smirks. "That's my girl."

"Your girl?"

"If I say it enough, will you give in and believe it too? I care too much to just walk away. I know I screwed up plenty of times this week. And I'll screw up more in the future, I'm sure.

I'm arrogant. I push boundaries. I get in trouble."

"Are you trying to win me over right now?"

"I'm not done." He runs his hands along my arms, and I swear I could melt right here. "I fight with people. I have an ugly past. I rarely learn from my mistakes the first time around. I don't realize the things I love most until it's too late. And I fall for girls I barely know who show up in my driveway nervous about a job interview."

"Girls?"

"One girl. And I want her to give me a chance."

I raise my eyebrows.

"*Another* chance. I might need a hundred more, but I think, deep down, this is what you want too—even if you're afraid to admit it."

"Now who's the one making assumptions?"

I see a dark gray Benz come up the driveway and stop near us. Mark's behind the wheel.

Devon could have left. He could have walked away from me, gone into any club, any bar, anywhere. He could have found any other girl to replace me in a second.

But he waited for me.

How many other times in life does another chance to do things right fall at your feet? I'd taken control inside with Keenly. I could do it again now.

But do I choose my head or my heart? Logic or a chance at love?

Like Maddie said, I want Devon. I should get Devon.

He brings his hand to my face and traces the contour of my jaw. His thumb grazes my lips. I want him. I should get him.

Turning to the car, he opens the door to the backseat. "Come with me."

"Where?"

"It doesn't matter. Anywhere you want. I just want to be with you."

I want you. I should get you.

My things are inside—my purse, my wallet, my phone. My car's in the driveway. My roommate will be looking for me.

Oh well.

I step past him and climb inside, my heart threatening to beat through my chest. Watching me through the open door, Devon seems almost surprised, as though he'd prepared to be rejected.

I try to keep a straight face, realizing, for the first time with him, I have the upper hand. "Well?" I say. "What are you waiting for?"

THE LUST LIST: DEVON STONE

SECOND CHANCES

MIRA BAILEE

Available Now

THE LUST LIST

The Lust List - Take Your Pick
They're the world's sexiest bachelors. The men of *ScandalLust* mag's infamous Lust List are young, wealthy, and, oh, did we mention? *Hot*.

When scandal follows them everywhere, there's no hiding from the cameras. They're irresistible, insatiable—and talented in all the right ways. Every woman wants them. But these playboys won't be easy to catch...

THE LUST LIST DEVON STONE

by MIRA BAILEE

FIRST TASTE
SECOND CHANCES
THIRD DEGREE
FOUR LETTERS

Acknowledgments

I couldn't be more grateful for those who helped bring *First Taste* to life:

Nova Raines, who boldly agreed to co-create NoMi Press and *The Lust List* universe with me. I appreciate your creativity and talent, your trust in me, and your passion for seeking new challenges.

Nicole Bailey at Proof Before You Publish for polishing my work into a shiny diamond.

Qamber Designs for their outstanding covers and creative services.

And to my family and friends, who've always been supportive, insisting I was awesome without ever needing proof.

About Mira Bailee

Mira Bailee, a beer-brewing librarian, has been writing leisurely, scholarly, and professionally for the past twenty years.

While she's always maintained a high standard of chaos in her daily routine, *The Lust List* allows her to pass on some of her hectic lifestyle to her characters. Her storytelling balances humor and pleasure with sincerity and conflict, providing a wild ride of human emotions.

In the past she studied filmmaking and screenwriting and determined what goes on behind the scenes is just as tantalizing as what's seen in front of the camera. This revelation is the basis for her inspiration for *The Lust List*.